I0590637

THE CREATIVE STRATEGIST

THE CREATIVE STRATEGIST

UNSTOPPABLE LIV BEAUFONT™ BOOK 11

SARAH NOFFKE

MICHAEL ANDERLE

This book is a work of fiction.

All of the characters, organizations, and events portrayed in this novel
are either products of the author's imagination or are used fictitiously.
Sometimes both.

Copyright © 2019 Sarah Noffke & Michael Anderle
Cover copyright © LMBPN Publishing
A Michael Anderle Production

LMBPN Publishing supports the right to free expression and the value of
copyright. The purpose of copyright is to encourage writers and artists
to produce the creative works that enrich our culture.

The distribution of this book without permission is a theft of the
author's intellectual property. If you would like permission to use
material from the book (other than for review purposes), please contact
support@lmbpn.com. Thank you for your support of the author's rights.

LMBPN Publishing
PMB 196, 2540 South Maryland Pkwy
Las Vegas, NV 89109

First US Edition, September 2019
Version 1.03, August 2020
eBook ISBN: 978-1-64202-441-8
Print ISBN: 978-1-64202-442-5

THE CREATIVE STRATEGIST TEAM

Thanks to the JIT Readers

Nicole Emens
Jeff Eaton
Dorothy Lloyd
Peter Manis
Deb Mader
Daniel Weigert
Angel LaVey
Larry Omans
Misty Roa

If I've missed anyone, please let me know!

Editor
The Skyhunter Editing Team

For Trudy.
The first day we met, you called me a tiger.
Still my favorite college class ever. And the one that flamed my
fire for writing.
— Sarah

To Family, Friends and
Those Who Love
to Read.
May We All Enjoy Grace
to Live the Life We Are
Called.
— Michael

Two red-faced demons ran straight at the low part of a roller coaster, leaping over the track with ease and landing on the other side, where the closed amusement park spread out for several acres. None of the lights were on, making it appear to be a ghost town, especially since it was deserted.

During the day, the Magic Playland attracted local mortal visitors with its rides, which, according to recent police reports, went too fast, moved on their own, and had carousel animals that talked.

The last demon, an especially ugly one, decided not to jump the coaster, but rather ran straight through the bottom, breaking apart many of the boards that held up the track, as it continued across the ground, following the other two demons.

"Well, I guess I won't be going on that ride now," Liv said, darting around the roller coaster track after deciding it was unwise for her to attempt to jump it the way the first two demons had. This detour put some distance between her and the demons she'd been hunting for the better part of ten minutes.

She wasn't worried about losing them, though, since she was with the one person who could find a needle in a haystack, or rather, a needle in a large amusement park—if that needle was a demon. Stefan Ludwig could find any demon anywhere if he merely focused. That was how he'd accidentally found these three demons hiding behind the concession stands at Magic Playland, drooling over the popcorn machine.

"I'm never eating popcorn again," Liv had remarked to Stefan as they sprinted after the demons through the park.

Stefan, who had slowed to retrieve his bow and arrow, caught up with her on the other side of the roller coaster. With a grace to amaze, he brought the bow up in one fluid movement, loaded the arrow, and fired, knocking the closest demon down. The beast would still need to be decapitated or otherwise dispatched with Bellator, but he was out for the moment.

"Since when do you eat popcorn?" he asked. He was by her side, wearing a slight grin, continuing the conversation like they hadn't been zigzagging through an amusement park just before.

"I've been known to," Liv said, watching as the two remaining demons split off.

"I thought if it didn't come loaded on tortilla chips, you didn't waste your time," he remarked.

She narrowed her eyes, watching the two demons and trying to decide which one she should go after. "What is it with you and demons? We can't go anywhere without them ruining our adventures."

"It's part of my charm," he teased. "I hope you don't mind. They will forever ruin every date we ever go on."

She flashed him a challenging smile. "I don't think I'd have it any other way."

Stefan bowed slightly to her. "And that's why you're the woman for me."

"Not yet, I'm not," she stated, watching as one of the demons boarded a carriage on the Ferris wheel.

"I know, I know," Stefan said, disappointment in his voice. "No dates until the dumb laws are changed."

The second demon glanced back at them before ducking into the Funhouse of Mirrors.

"Seriously?" Liv sighed. "Are they totally trying to mess with us?"

Stefan laughed. "I do believe they are. You go after the dummy who got on the unmoving Ferris wheel. I'll take his ugly brother, who will look even uglier in the funhouse."

Liv was about to agree when the bulbs covering the Ferris wheel lit up, illuminating that part of the dark amusement park. Suddenly the wheel began to move, taking the demon higher.

Liv groaned. "You just had to say something about the Ferris wheel not moving, didn't you?"

"Yeah, you better take Two-Horns McUgly," Stefan said, indicating the funhouse. "I'll go after his more attractive brother."

The demon on the Ferris wheel wasn't attractive by anyone's standards, ever. However, his red face was void of pockmarks, and his bald head wasn't adorned by two gnarled horns like the other demon. He had soulless black eyes like all demons, but in comparison to most, he wasn't atrocious.

"Yeah, you're better off getting him with the bow and arrow," Liv said, pulling Bellator from its sheath and twirling it at her side like it was a baton.

"I'll catch up with you in a minute," Stefan stated, striding toward the Ferris wheel. The demon was almost at the top now.

"Sounds good," Liv said, walking up to the demon lying face-down in the dirt with Stefan's arrow protruding from his back. He was beginning to move again, trying to get his hands underneath him. Liv whirled Bellator one more time like she was a flag bearer in a parade. When she strode by the demon, she casually stuck the sword into its back, making it scream. It collapsed back to the ground, lifeless.

Liv yanked Bellator from its back, holding it at the ready as she neared the funhouse.

Liv wasn't only there because mortals had been put in danger on the rides, which were obviously powered by magical tech. Actually, the Magic Playland hadn't even been on the council's radar yet. That was because the magician who ran it was unregistered, and had used a lot of magical tech to cover up his affairs.

It was because of John Carraway that Liv knew about Sid Encore, one of the lead members of the Renegades. He'd been spying on the rebel group, finding useful information, such as where bad magicians were running illegal operations.

The Renegades didn't want the House of Fourteen intervening in their affairs, and the Magic Playland was a prime example of why. They wanted to do things that were wrong and put mortals in danger. But today, this amusement park was getting shut down as soon as they located Sid Encore—and disposed of the three demons who apparently also called this place home.

"Never a dull moment," Liv said, sliding into the funhouse with Bellator at the ready. She knew the demon was still in there and hadn't slipped out the back, not only because she could hear its ragged breath, but also because she could smell its disgusting odor.

She glanced into the mirror across from her and started. It took her a moment to realize the image was her, only aged by several decades. This place was full of illegal magic that had no place in the mortal world. Even if mortals were learning that magic was real, they didn't need it shoved into their faces without warning.

There had to be parameters, which was what the House was currently working on. For unsuspecting mortals, visiting the Magic Playland was like going into a wax museum and finding out all the figures were alive. Mortals shouldn't be deceived. That was wrong. Things had to be labeled appropriately. If they were enhanced with magic, then they had to state that.

Of course, anyone who was a part of the Renegades was violently opposed to regulations. They saw it as an infringement on their freedom, but that was probably because they were the ones tricking mortals and laughing about the whole thing. Liv was excited to put a stop to their bullying.

Sneaking around a corner, Liv faced a mirror that made her appear exceptionally tall.

Well, that's *obviously a trick of the eye,* she thought

A flash of red darted behind her. She spun around, finding nothing but a dozen mirrors at different angles, making a strange hallway across the funhouse. Liv laughed, amused by her odd predicament.

She traversed in the direction she'd seen the demon cross, her eyes darting back and forth, watching for any more signs of the beast. In her peripheral vision, she caught something and brought Bellator up, ready to strike. The only thing she saw was a figure of herself, blinking.

The image wasn't distorted like the others. This Liv matched her exactly, showing her long, unkempt blonde hair and billowing black cape. Then the figure stepped forward, although the real Liv Beaufont remained still.

"Aren't you tired of always doing what you're told?" the fake Liv asked.

Oh, man, I hate this Sid Encore guy already, Liv thought, not daring to answer the illusion of her. It strode around her, getting entirely too close for her liking.

"When we allow others to control us, we give them our power," the fake Liv continued.

She caught a flicker of red behind the illusion. It was fast, but she was certain she knew where it had gone. It was just on the other side of the closest partition.

A sudden idea occurred to her. *It was time to dance.*

The fake Liv traced around her, stopping when it was in front. She opened her mouth to say something, but Real Liv cut her off.

"Rebelling against authority is the only way to show them you can't be beat," Liv stated, beginning to circle the illusion, appearing as stoic as it was. It was like the cup trick street vendors did. If she was fast and convincing enough, no one could tell the difference between them, especially a stupid demon.

The illusion froze, Liv's strange change in behavior throwing it off. Deceptive spells like this fed on the unknowing individual, reciting a canned speech. However, her unexpected words interrupted its programming, causing it to freeze.

"If we all rise up against the power holding us down, we will win," Liv continued, stopping when she was on the other side of the illusion.

She had Bellator in the air when the demon sprang out from behind the partition. The monster went to wrap its arms around the illusion of Liv but fell forward, catching nothing but air. Liv brought her sword horizontally in a swift, clean movement, slicing through her image and the demon's midsection and spilling black blood all over the floor. The demon screamed, its eyes widening like it was surprised and offended by the trick. Then it crumpled to the ground, falling straight on its face.

CHAPTER TWO

"And strangely, this isn't the most bizarre situation I've ever caught you in," Stefan said, striding up from behind her, his bow slung over his back.

Fake Liv blinked impassively ahead as the demon's blood inched forward on the floor, nearing Real Liv's boots

"Well, Mr. Ludwig," Liv said, turning to face him, "I hope you *never* catch me in a predictable situation."

He nodded, checking himself out in a mirror that portrayed him as tremendously distorted. "You know, even in these messed-up reflections, I'm still rather handsome."

Liv pointed her finger and cracked the mirror. "Really? Then why did that happen?"

He spun to face her with a clever grin on his face. "Oh, Ms. Beaufont, you wound me. Don't you know, I'm only looking for a little attention from you? Do I really have to fish for compliments?"

Liv drew closer to him and put her finger on his chest. She leaned in, inhaling deeply, then brought her eyes up to meet his. "Yes, you absolutely do."

As soon as the mock disappointment flicked to his eyes, Liv swerved around him, striding toward the exit. "So I suppose you got Ugly's cousin-brother? Or whatever he was?"

"I did, my lady," Stefan said, easily catching up with her in a few swift steps.

"Well, then I suppose we had better find this Sid guy so I can throw a candy apple straight at his face."

"About that," Stefan said in a whisper. "I'm all up for punishing this guy, but…"

When Liv turned to face him, they were nearly nose to nose, her staring up as he stared down. "What?"

"Well, I found something a bit disconcerting that I think you should see," he replied.

"Besides mirror images that come alive and encourage children to rebel against society?" Liv questioned.

He nodded.

Liv rolled her eyes, wondering for a moment why she hadn't been born to an insurance salesman and lived a normal life. Then she reminded herself that anyone presently living on planet Earth wasn't experiencing anything normal anymore.

"Here, it's out this way," Stefan said, tugging on her cape and leading her out into the night air.

"Based on how you're moving," Liv began, following him, "I'm guessing you know where Sid Encore is."

He nodded over his shoulder. "He's about a hundred yards behind us, inspecting the damage to his roller coaster. I don't think he knows we're here yet, which is perfect."

"So why are we running the opposite direction?" Liv asked. "I thought we were supposed to be bringing him in?"

"We are," Stefan agreed. "However, what I found might change things."

"Like how?"

"Like, we bargain with him first," Stefan answered.

Liv halted. "This guy is despicable, tricking mortals and especially young children. Who knows the kind of damage he's caused? And you want to bargain with him?"

Stefan grabbed her hand, hauling her toward the carousel. "I know exactly what type of damage he's caused." He urged her closer to the carousel, which was adorned with magnificent statues of unicorns, all tethered to poles that ran through the top and bottom of the ride.

Liv turned with an incredulous expression. "When did you become such a pansy, Ludwig, wanting to bargain with villains instead of taking them in and ensuring they are punished?"

He blinked at her, unruffled. "Take a closer look at the animals there."

Liv turned, studying the unicorns. The craftsmanship was incredible. She'd heard from the reports that Sid Encore had magicked them to come alive, making the guests nearly fall off the moving carousel. And then she noticed what Stefan meant. A gasp fell from her mouth, and she stumbled back. Threw her hand toward Stefan, grabbed his shirt, and pulled him close to her face.

"The unicorns are real," she said in a rush.

He nodded, his eyes darting between her and the unicorns, which she could see were moving minutely. That was because they were imprisoned, and were desperately trying to free themselves from the spell that had them captured.

Liv released her hand from Stefan's shirt, allowing everything he had said to sink in. "And if we capture Sid Encore, he won't be willing to help us."

Stefan nodded triumphantly.

"But if we bargain for his freedom in exchange for the unicorns, he will release them," she continued.

"And that's when we actually take the good-for-nothing-scoundrel in, locking his magic for the rest of his life," Stefan stated defiantly.

Liv smiled, realizing what a genius plan it was. Whatever magic the magician had used to trap the unicorns was powerful, and chances were that the one who had trapped them was the one who needed to release them. Or at least, by the time the House figured out how the complicated spell worked, it might be too late for the unicorns. Also, locking the magician's magic could cause all sorts of problems. Sometimes that backfired, harming anything they spelled, which would instantly kill the unicorns.

"So we have to bargain with the revolting jerk," Liv said, looking in the direction of the roller coaster.

Stefan flashed her a confident smile. "And I know of no one better for the job than the girl who stands before me now."

CHAPTER THREE

As casually as if she were strolling to meet a friend, Liv walked up to the grumbling magician who was studying the damage to the structure of his roller coaster. He caught sight of her as she neared, lowering his hands to his hips and narrowing his eyes at her.

"Are you the one who did this?" Sid Encore asked, his voice strangely high-pitched for a male.

He wore a pencil mustache and goatee. On his head was a top hat that had a masquerade mask around it, and on his hands, he wore a pair of dirty white gloves.

"Nope," Liv said, ducking through the damaged roller coaster. "It was demons. Did you know you had a few living behind your concession stand?"

"They aren't a problem," Sid stated, giving her a scolding look with his dark eyes.

So he did know. "Except that they feed off mortals' energy and also take over magicians and other magical creatures, turning them into soul-sucking beings."

"They don't bother me."

"Because you offer up the mortals for them to feed upon," Liv guessed.

"Who are you?" Sid Encore asked.

"I'm Liv Beaufont, a Warrior for the House of Fourteen," she stated proudly. "And I'm here because I've been notified about the demon problem."

Sid straightened. Tensed. Took a breath and shrugged. "Yeah, well, what can you do about demons?"

Liv inched in closer to the evil magician. "Well, like with all law-breakers, I kill them, avoiding protocol. Paperwork is a bitch. I'd rather just pretend they got hit by a train during a chase, and..." She copied his shrug. "What am I to do if those dummies hit a moving vehicle or my sword when the law was after them?"

"So you came after my demons," Sid said casually, looking at the gaping hole in his roller coaster's foundation.

"Yes, and now they are dead."

Sid spun, looking one way and then another. "Are you serious? What? Where? You did that? On your own?"

Liv twirled her hair like a schoolgirl. "Well, there were three of them and one of me, so it didn't take long."

"B-b-but..."

She stepped forward, stabbing her finger into the puny magician's chest. "And while ending those monsters, I noticed that you happen to have other illegal magic tech, too."

He held up his hands. "If you're going to challenge me on this, I'll—"

Liv snapped her fingers. "I just took care of your portal

magic. It's been turned off," she lied. "Try getting out of here."

He could have tried, but given the way he was trembling, he didn't have the courage. Many thought the House of Fourteen had ways of disabling portals, certain spells, and even glamours. It was false, just well-placed rumors meant to keep the law-breakers from getting away with too much.

"I really don't care about the magic tech," Liv stated matter-of-factly. "All I want is for you to release the unicorns from the carousel."

"The unicorns?" Sid Encore protested. "But they are my…"

The punishing look on Liv's face halted any more words from him.

"I c-c-can't," he stuttered.

"You can't?" she questioned.

"The unicorns were given to me by a friend, and if I… I can't," Sid repeated, not looking at her.

"If you don't release the unicorns, I'll have no choice but to shut you down," Liv stated, desperately hoping he believed her. Yes, she *could* shut him down, and he absolutely knew it. What he didn't know was that she needed him to release the unicorns, or they'd be in danger. However, something in the way he kept glancing at the rafters above them in the roller coaster made her doubt that he was taking her seriously.

"I understand," he said, but strangely, he didn't seem to mean it.

Liv was about to try another approach when he sprang, landing in the roller coaster cart above them.

The good thing was that he seemed to believe Liv had frozen his portal magic, but the bad thing was that he'd landed in what she now realized was a getaway-car on a roller coaster. It started forward immediately upon him landing in it, quickly heading down a steep slope and away.

"Oh, hell, nah," Liv stated, portaling and landing on the nearest docking station the roller coaster would come to. She stepped out of the portal just as the cart climbed the hill to where she was stationed.

This was just a getaway technique. Liv knew it wouldn't last long. Sid Encore was working on another way out. She just didn't know what, and that was what worried her the most.

When the first cart neared the top, Liv jumped into it and climbed to where Sid was sitting at the back. He caught sight of her, his eyes growing wide with nervousness.

She lost her balance many times, knocked back and forth as the train churned forward. Liv held onto something with every step, and she wondered why Sid Encore appeared mostly relaxed as he regarded her from the last cart. Then the first part of the coaster dipped over the edge and they began racing over the tallest incline, speeding down, making her cheeks stream backward. Her hair rippled around her face as she held on for dear life.

Liv couldn't move. Just trying to stay anchored to the roller coaster was enough. At any moment, she was going to be thrown to her death. She just knew it. The track slung her to the side and she locked her foot under a seat, hoping that would keep her from flying halfway across the amusement park.

The coaster slowed as it continued on a straightaway, giving Liv a chance to catch her breath.

A quick glance at Sid Encore told her he wasn't concerned at all. He was actually holding something up with a victorious grin on his pale face, and she narrowed her eyes, trying to make it out. Then, as the train she was riding sped up and his cart slowed, she realized what it was.

Sid Encore was holding the pin that had locked his cart to the rest of the train.

Wait, what? Liv's eyes widened.

He was stalled several yards behind her, not slinging around the track like the other carts.

If that wasn't enough to alarm her, Liv noticed the strange movement of his mouth. She recognized the incantation. It was one she'd used before. He was trying to freeze her in place. Liv looked over her shoulder and realized with horror that she was about to come full circle, in a way. The next incline ended at exactly the place the demon had crashed through. Liv was absolutely certain the track wouldn't be able to support the train, causing a deadly crash.

She tried to move but realized she was locked into the car. Sid's spell had worked. She couldn't portal away. She couldn't even move her mouth to say a single incantation. This kind of magic was strong. It wouldn't last long, but it didn't need to. Soon the cart of the coaster would spill over the edge of the hill, sending her to her doom.

Liv caught sight of Stefan on the ground. He was exactly in the place he'd said he'd be, standing squarely in the center of the roller coaster. His crazed look told her he knew something was wrong.

Sid Encore jumped out of his cart, which had slowed almost to a stop. Quickly he climbed over the edge, using the wooden slats of the structure to get down to the ground from less than a story up.

Liv's eyes, the only part of her that could move, darted to Stefan. He'd pulled his bow, aimed, and within a second, shot. Liv heard a loud yelp of pain, followed by a thud. Stefan disappeared, running for the roller coaster.

Liv couldn't see anything else below since the figures were out of her line of sight. The cranking of the coaster told her she was nearing the top. It was only a matter of seconds before the cart she wasn't strapped into spilled over the edge. Either she'd be slung off since she was unable to hold on, or the cart would crash when it hit the damaged track. Neither possibility left her with any hope of surviving.

CHAPTER FOUR

The air seemed to still around Liv, almost like the god of the wind knew she was about to plummet to her death. In the distance, she could see the Ferris wheel, still lit up and circling. It illuminated the carousel close by.

Liv's heart sank as she realized how badly she'd erred. A loud crack under her cart was followed by silence, and she felt her body tip to the side. It was the brief moment before the coaster tipped forward, barreling down a hill. Usually, park-goers would throw up their hands and yell with excitement, enjoying the rush. There would be none of that for Liv.

She was about to close her eyes, shutting away the terror building in her mind, when she noticed the animals on the carousel moving. Not a little bit, like before. Rather, they were hopping off the machine. Frolicking, the way a pony does when freed after being confined for a long period of time.

Her fingers twitched, and she jerked her head to the side. That might have been a bad idea. It was like looking down while hanging from a skyscraper. Below was the dangerous dip that led to the damaged track, and that was exactly where she was headed. But she was free. She was moving! Stefan had done it! He'd had Sid release her and free the unicorns!

But it might be too late for her. The coaster tipped fully over the crest and started racing down the hill. Liv shot forward, nearly flying out of the cart. Her hand caught the bar just in time. Holding on tight wouldn't save her from the fall she was about to take, though.

With the wind blasting her in the face, she put all her focus into creating a portal. There was no time for anything else. She knew it. Stefan, watching from the ground, had to know it. He couldn't save her. Like many times in her life, Liv had to save herself.

The glow of the portal illuminated in front of her. It was like looking into a mirror, and that was for the best since she didn't want to see where she was headed if she didn't get off the cart. Liv didn't know how she was going to step through the portal in front of her. That was usually how she did it, but with the wind barreling past her face, she could hardly breathe, let alone walk.

With all her might, she was holding onto the seat in front of her. She considered picking up her foot and climbing, but she wasn't sure how to manage it. And then the dilemma was settled for her; the cart hit the broken track, knocking her forward violently. Liv tumbled head-first, somersaulting through the portal and rolling onto the soft grass below.

Jumping to her feet, Liv looked up in time to see the train

she'd been riding on plummeting several stories and crashing to the ground. The carts exploded, sending debris everywhere and making Liv shield her eyes. A fiery burst followed, and Liv wrapped her hands over her head as she ducked away from it. She kept herself covered until the heat dissipated.

"Someone wanted you dead," Stefan said when she rose to her feet.

She took in the rising flames eating at the boards of the roller coaster. "Yeah, someone must have had enough time to magic up some explosions."

"Well, he won't be doing much of that for a while." Stefan pointed to where Sid Encore was sitting in the grass, trying to reach the puncture wound in his back where the arrow had struck. He was jerking his head back and forth.

"So you got him to release the unicorns?" Liv asked, glancing in the direction of the carousel.

"Well, an arrow in the back and a sword held to the throat helps with negotiations," Stefan said, pointing at Sid and making ropes tie around his hands at his back.

"Thanks for saving me," Liv said to Stefan, checking her limbs to ensure they were all there.

Stefan shook his head. "I didn't do much. You're the one who created a portal on a racing roller coaster. I hope you get that that's pretty insane."

Liv shrugged. She didn't. What was the protocol on that? All she knew was what it took to survive, and she was grateful she had the right kind of people at her side to help her to do it.

Sid continued to struggle in his bindings. "Oh, man, I'm

just trying to fix what you did to me! There's a hole in my back!"

"It's a flesh wound," Stefan replied. "And we'll have the best of the best at the House of the Fourteen prison look after your tiny cut."

Sid threw his head to one side and then the other. "This isn't fair. I can't lose my unicorns and my amusement park."

Liv, her attention still on the flames consuming the roller coaster, directed her focus to the evil magician instead. "You should have thought about that before you used illegal magic tech to enhance your park. And enslaved unicorns."

Sid fussed in his restraints. "If the House would just leave us alone, this would never have been an issue."

Liv laughed, both feeling the adrenaline of surviving another near-death experience and the victory that came when she won. "That's the thing, Sid. The House will never leave you alone. We are more powerful than ever before, and we're not allowing injustice to rule. Not as long as there are those who care about the world you want to abuse."

Stefan hauled Sid to his feet and opened a portal outside the House of Fourteen.

"What you don't get is the world outside of magicians isn't worth protecting," Sid stated. "It's our oyster."

Liv shook her head. "Not on my watch, it isn't."

She winked at Stefan, and that seemed to be all he needed to dutifully trot the criminal through the portal to a place where he'd be tried and held for his crimes.

CHAPTER FIVE

"Well, that was highly entertaining to watch," Plato said, materializing beside Liv once she stepped through the portal beside the dusty highway. Liam's barbeque restaurant was crowded, from the looks of the parking lot.

"I almost died," Liv grumbled, fanning dust away from her face.

"I saw that," Plato stated matter-of-factly.

"But thankfully, I didn't."

"Thankfully," he said.

"I mean, you might have stepped in to save me if need be," she said, watching as locals trotted out of the restaurant, looking happy and full. Most of them were magical creatures since Liam's place was popular with gnomes, fairies, and other types.

"You never want to count on that," Plato said almost in a whisper.

Liv jerked her head down and stared at him. She'd been

baiting him into this conversation, hoping to get him to reveal the secret he was holding onto and promising to reveal. "And why is that?"

He shrugged. "You just don't."

Liv sighed. The lynx was a vault. If he didn't want to share, there was little she could do to get him to open up.

"You know what I love about Texas?" Liv asked, putting her hands on her hips and leaning back, taking in the giant blue sky.

"That it's legal to carry a weapon?" Plato guessed.

Liv slid her cape back to reveal a tiny bit of Bellator. "That's never a problem for me. I carry no matter what state I'm in."

"Is it that the weather is like a crazy person with multiple personalities? You never know what you're going to get?" Plato asked.

Liv shook her head. "No, that's not it."

"Is it that the word 'y'all' can be broken up into three syllables, and is a staple in all conversations?"

"Nope. It's that in Texas, you can watch your dog run away for three days." Liv sighed, looking out at the flat earth that went on for miles and miles.

"You don't have a dog," Plato said dryly.

"Oh, forget it," Liv said, ambling toward the door.

Rory and Bermuda had been able to use their magic to hide Sophia's dragon egg from the Elite, but it wasn't going to last for long. The best solution was to move the egg to a place where the dragon was content, which apparently wasn't in her apartment. If Simon or Nick or whatever Sophia named the dragon was comfortable, it would stop registering for the Elite, the secret society of dragon riders.

Liv knew that one day, Sophia and Tom would have to leave to join their own. But not yet. She needed just a little longer with her sister before she grew up too rapidly, fighting and doing things that made Liv's job as a Warrior seem ordinary.

That was why she'd come to Texas—to recruit a giant who could help with transport. The restaurant was close to the Magic Playland, so pairing up the adventures seemed like a no-brainer.

Even though the egg was only three feet tall, it was growing fast and weighed an incredible amount. Rory might be able to pick it up on his own, but if he stumbled or something happened, he could drop it and the egg would be damaged, causing all sorts of problems.

Giants were the ideal magical creatures for handling the dragon egg. Their magic subdued it, helping keep it off the Elite's radar. Also, since giants couldn't be riders, the dragon never felt pressured by them.

"So what's the plan?" Plato asked, following Liv to the door.

"I'm just going to mosey on in here and casually grab a booth," she answered.

"And then what?"

"And then I'm going to ask Liam if I can borrow his daughter for an important top-secret task," she stated confidently.

"Good idea," Plato said, his tone teeming with sarcasm. "I see no way this will go wrong."

Liv pulled open the door to the dark restaurant, letting the bright Texas sun spill into the place. Everyone turned and looked at her, their eyes lingering on her as rude glares flicked to their faces.

"Oh, hell, no!" Liam, the owner of the restaurant, yelled. The giant marched from the back straight over to Liv, his face red. "I don't want you in here! Remember? I told you that."

Liv held up her hands, faking a smile. "Look, I don't have the chicken that caused you so much trouble with me."

He shook his head. "Doesn't matter. Wherever you go, trouble follows."

"I sort of feel you're stereotyping," Liv said, pretending to be hurt. "Is it because I'm a woman? Or a blonde?" She gasped loudly. "Is it because I'm a Virgo?"

He scoffed, not falling for this. "No, it's because you're a Warrior for the House of Fourteen." Liam leaned over, nearly having to bend in half to reach Liv's ear. "My patrons come here to get away from things. They like their privacy, and if some police officer is known to be hanging around, then they aren't going to enjoy my establishment so much."

Liv glanced around the giant, which wasn't easy to do. "Sounds like you've got some law-breakers in here. Maybe I should do a little quality control."

Liam stepped to the side, blocking her view. "You'll do no such thing. My customers are good. They just want to eat and not be judged."

Liv sighed. "Well, that's a relief. That's exactly why I'm here. I'm totally off-duty, and just wanted a place where I can kick back and have the finest barbeque in the continental United States."

Liam narrowed his eyes at her, apparently trying to decide how authentic she was being. "You're off-duty?"

"That's right," Liv stated. "And it's been a hell of a day, so if someone comes in here causing problems, you better believe you're going to have to save yourself. There is zero way I'm going to wrangle any bad guys after the night that I've had."

Tilting his head to the side, the giant studied her. "So you just came in to eat?"

"Well, and drink, too, if that's all right with you? I could use a beer or three."

This seemed to relax him. "Okay, fine. Follow me." Liam led her to a booth at the back, which strangely was mostly out of view of the others. A table of gnomes hushed as she walked by, and a group of leprechauns all stuck their hands under the table as she passed. Liv pretended to yawn as if she wasn't the least bit interested in their activity. She was taking notes, though. Damn leprechauns were known for scamming, and she was close to figuring out what the little runts were up to.

"Here you go," Liam said, holding his hand out to the booth. The lights over it dimmed suddenly.

"It's a bit dark, isn't it?" she questioned.

"It's this or nothing."

Liv took a seat, drumming her hands on the table. "You have a menu?"

He crossed his thick arms over his chest. "No. We have barbeque and sides. What do you want?"

"Hmmm," Liv said, trying to look into the back and spot the giantess named Matilda. "I'm not sure. I might need a minute. Will you send over the waitress in a bit?"

He shook his head. "I'll wait for your order."

Liv silently groaned. The grumpy giant wasn't going to make this easy. "Well, I'm keto, so although I can eat lots of meat, I need to watch my sugars. How many carbs are in a serving of your barbeque sauce?"

"I don't know," he replied at once.

"And can you substitute lettuce for the bun if I get the pulled pork sandwich?"

He shook his head. "No."

Liv thought for a moment, trying to figure out how to throw the giant off. "I have a nut allergy. Only to pecans, though. You don't by chance use pecan wood to roast your meat, do you?"

"I-I'm not sure."

Liv's eyes shifted back and forth. "I wonder if someone in the back might know? I wouldn't want to have an allergic reaction in front of all of your customers. That would cause a scene."

For a moment, Liam looked like he might reach across the table and grab her by the neck. Instead, he sighed and lumbered toward the back.

"Oh, and I'll take a bucket of beers!" Liv yelled after him. "Please!"

Yes, Liam was going to kill her, but it would be okay if she got Matilda to help. Quickly she stood up and looked around the restaurant for the giantess. Anyone who noticed her searching ducked, avoiding eye contact. The leprechauns scowled. Liv grimaced right back, growling slightly.

Just when she thought she might have shown up on the

waitress's day off, the beautiful giant materialized, carrying a tray of cornbread. Liv remembered she was attractive, in comparison to most giants. Her features weren't too big or small, and they complimented each other. Her blonde hair was pulled back in pigtails, making her appear young although she was easily the same age as Rory, in her mid-thirties. Giants didn't have the privilege of growing old gracefully like other magical races, probably due to their size.

"Over here!" Liv yelled, waving at the giantess.

Maddie set a tray of cornbread on the table in front of her and glanced at Liv. She smiled, which was incredibly rare for a giant. Without having to be prompted further, she hurried over.

"Well, hello, Warrior Beaufont. It's great to see you. My papa said he's waiting on you directly, but is there something I can help you with?"

"Oh," Liv said, thinking quickly. "I was really hoping you'd be my waitress."

Maddie gave her a pained expression. "Sorry, my papa seems to want to ensure you have his expert service. And I do have all these other tables to attend to, so I'll just be on my way."

"Cornbread!" Liv yelled, stopping the giantess before she could leave.

Maddie halted. "What's that? You want cornbread?"

Liv nodded like a child begging for seconds.

"Sure, here you go," Maddie said, lying a basket of steaming-hot cornbread on the table. "Good to see you. Enjoy your meal."

"Actually, I need your help," Liv said in a rush, looking around for Liam. "I've got something important that my giant friend and I need to transport."

"Do you mean Rory? The giant you brought in here last time?" Maddie asked, her face blossoming with curiosity.

Liv nodded. "Yes, and I need another giant. I was hoping that since you're curious about magicians, the House, and the West Coast, you'd consider the offer."

Maddie appeared pained. "I wished I could. That sounds very tempting, but I have my job here."

"Right," Liv said, drawing out the word, trying to come up with another option. "It's just that my little sister really needs help with a project, and I was thinking…"

She was hoping the little sister card would persuade the giantess, but her features didn't shift. When Liv didn't say anything further, Maddie simply offered an apologetic smile.

"I really wished I could help, but Papa needs me, and my family comes first," she said.

Liv deflated, hanging her head.

"Maddie, what are you doing over here?" Liam nearly yelled, rushing over to the table.

Liv didn't even bother to look up.

"Sorry, Papa. It's just that Warrior Beaufont asked for cornbread," Maddie explained. "And she very thoughtfully offered me a job."

"Did she?" Liam growled.

Liv looked up, guiltily. "Yes, about that wood? Is it pecan?"

Maddie giggled, another thing one never saw a giant

do. "Don't worry, Papa. I told her I had responsibilities here."

"What is the meaning of this, Warrior Beaufont?" Liam asked, his face so red it appeared to be covered in barbeque sauce.

"Sorry, Liam," Liv said in a rush. "It's just that Rory and I need help transporting something. It's for my sister. Bermuda says that we need another giant for it to be successful, and I just thought—"

"Do you mean, Bermuda Laurens?" Liam asked, his anger turning to intrigue.

Liv paused. "Why, yes, I do."

Liam ran his hands over his chin, appearing astonished. "Of course. That's Rory's mum. I didn't make the connection."

"You know Bermuda?" Liv asked.

"Do I?" Liam said. "We were childhood friends. Lost touch, of course. I've been here with Maddie, and she's been...well, traveling the globe for her book. Smart woman. As smart as they come. I'm surprised you are close to that woman."

"Bermuda and I?" Liv asked and then laughed. "We are pretty much besties."

"And she needs Maddie's help?" Liam asked.

"Well, she needs a giant's help, and as you know, there's the festival on the mainland, and therefore not a lot of giants around to offer assistance."

Liam nodded, seeming to understand at once. "I don't want to let Bermuda down. We were once really close. Like sister and brother. She didn't mention me?"

Liv dropped her chin. "She did. Of course, she did.

Spoke about you fondly, but she didn't want to push you to help. I thought I could simply ask Maddie and she'd do it. We didn't want to impose."

"Impose?" Liam said, lightening up quite a bit. "I've been looking for a way to pay Bermuda back for the thing she did at the Rock of Gibraltar."

"And this could be that," Liv stated. "But again, we don't want to impose."

Liam waved her off, taking another tray of cornbread from Maddie's hand. "Not at all. For Bermuda, I'm happy to loan Maddie." He looked at his daughter. "I daresay you could probably use a break from the restaurant."

"Are you sure, Papa?" Maddie asked, fussing with the end of one of her pigtails. "I don't want to leave you."

He shook his head adamantly. "It's totally fine. I insist. If Bermuda Laurens needs you, I want you to help. And although I'm unsure about this one." He indicated to Liv not so discreetly, "I trust you with Bermuda. We grew up together."

Liv looked over her shoulder like Liam might mean someone else.

"Thanks, Papa. I'm so excited. I get to go on a West Coast adventure," Maddie exclaimed with a slight squeal, throwing her arms around her father.

He blushed before pulling away from his daughter.

Liv stood, brushing off her cape. "Well, I guess we should be off, then."

"So you didn't come in here for food then, did you?" Liam asked with a scrutinizing gaze.

"I did, but I just remembered I'm vegan as well," Liv answered. "Do you have any tofu?"

Liam sighed, shaking his head at her. "Don't let anything happen to my daughter, Warrior Beaufont, or I'll have you roasted."

Liv saluted. "Don't worry, I'll have her home by curfew. Pinky promise."

CHAPTER SIX

Talon Sinclair stuck his head out of the Black Void, looking around the House for the first time in a century. It was different than he recalled, and yet the same. The Door of Reflection was as he remembered from the day Bernard Beaufont had created it. That hadn't been an easy bit of magic to do. The hallway was covered in gold, and to his horror, statues of the Mortal Seven lined one side. That meant they were growing stronger within the House.

As Talon knew, the corridor surrounding the void was deserted. He'd suspected that before daring to look out of the place he'd called home all those years. The Black Void wasn't pleasant, but it was concealed, and that was important. No one but his relatives could see it, keeping his presence secret.

Hearing someone approach, he pulled his head back, growing dizzy from venturing that far outside the void. It had kept him secure, even when his magical reserves were low. It had kept him hidden. And most importantly, it had given him a place to feed off the House's energy, growing stronger for the day he'd rise to full power.

"What did you see?" Kayla asked, picking at her finger-nails and appearing utterly bored.

"Nothing of importance," he said, sweeping back across the place that had been his sanctuary and was slowly starting to suffocate him. He needed to leave the Black Void soon, but not until Papa Creola was gone.

"So, the rest of the Mortal Seven?" Kayla began, flicking her white hair out of her face.

"Yes, why aren't you going after them now instead of being here?" Talon asked, his sunbeam eyes sweeping the floor but not really seeing as he thought.

"Because I don't know which one to go after? There are five families left. How do I know which one to target before Olivia Beaufont tries to cut me off?" Kayla asked.

Talon spun and stared straight at the girl before him. Unlike Alder, she didn't flinch from the brightness of his eyes. "Why do you need me to do everything for you? Just pick a family and go after them."

"Fine," Kayla said noncommittally. "And meanwhile?"

"And meanwhile, what?" he asked.

"What are *you* doing?" she dared to ask.

"I'm spying on the House of Seven's activity," he stated.

"By sticking your head out every day?" she asked, a laugh in her voice.

He shot her a wicked look. "I'm strong enough to hear different conversations going on in the House."

"But not strong enough to take your rightful place, is that right?"

Talon was about done with this descendant who didn't

have the proper respect for him. "I've told you, as long as Father Time is out there, I can't rise to full power."

"Which means, neither can I," she stated. "I'm a much better Warrior than a Councilor."

Because Talon had used a great deal of dark magic, the tree in the chamber had erased Kayla's name when Olivia Beaufont thought she killed the girl. That task, as well as waking an ancient beast, had depleted him of much of his power.

"I've stirred a beast who will draw Father Time out of hiding," Talon said.

"Oh, like the SandMan, or having the pirates steal his hourglass?" Kayla questioned in a taunting voice.

"No, not like that!" Talon roared. "Like a monster that will challenge and kill someone he won't want to die. A magical creature he sympathizes with a great deal because they share similar burdens."

"So you're not going to draw out Father Time, but rather hurt someone he cares about, hoping that works?" Kayla asked, doubt in her voice.

"Yes!" Talon roared. "Why? It's a good plan. He's the only one who can save this creature once their life is compromised. I'm certain he won't let them die. It will work. Once he's out of hiding, we'll swoop in and kill him."

Kayla shrugged, kicking at the wall. "If you say so."

Talon had had enough. He directed his attention at Kayla, and using only a fraction of his power, he knocked her to the floor, a gut-wrenching scream falling out of her mouth as her head hit it.

After much labored breathing, she whimpered, crawling forward, her fingernails clawing into the cement.

"Wh-wh-what was that?" she cried, drool spilling from her mouth as she tried to push herself back up.

"Don't ever disrespect me," Talon commanded, taking a seat on his throne of snakes and lizards.

"Y-y-yes, master. I'm sorry."

CHAPTER SEVEN

Sophia had Pickles in her lap when Liv entered with Maddie. The giantess turned into a baby-talking preschool-teacher-type at the sight of the chimera.

"Who's a big lion with a beautiful heart?" she asked the dog, stooping to pet him on the head. "*You* are. It's *you*."

Liv and John exchanged curious expressions as Sophia laughed, watching the dog lick Maddie's face.

"Ummm, you *can* see that he's a chimera?" Liv asked, not having given Maddie many details about what she had been recruited for. To her surprise, Maddie didn't seem to care. She simply stared around wide-eyed as Liv led her through the streets of West Hollywood toward John's shop.

"The guys pushing the carts, what are they selling again?" Maddie had asked, struggling to keep up with Liv since she kept stopping to admire the displays in the store windows. It was the opposite of when she walked with Rory. He was always bent on getting to his destination as quickly as possible with no detours, and one of his strides equaled three of Liv's.

Liv snickered. She hadn't answered the question the first time. "They are homeless. They aren't selling anything."

"Oh," Maddie said, seeming to choke on the word. "Then the carts are their…"

Liv nodded, giving the giantess an apologetic expression. Why did she have to be the one to educate her?

"Well, we have to do something." She reached into her pocket and pulled out a few coins. "Papa gave me his credit card for emergencies, but I think I have some dollars in here somewhere."

Liv grabbed Maddie by the arm and tugged her forward. "We aren't giving them money."

"Why?" Maddie complained. "The one back there looked really hungry. I would be too if I lived on the streets. Do you think he needs a shower? Maybe he could take one at your place."

"He can't, and we don't give money to the beggars because it doesn't solve the underlying problem," Liv explained.

"But Papa always says, 'On a full stomach, almost any problem can be solved.' Maybe all these homeless people need is a good meal," Maddie reasoned.

Liv tilted her head to the side, wanting to enjoy this moment of pure innocence before she ripped it all away. She opened her mouth to say something, then thought better of it, shaking her head. "Why don't you and Rory discuss strategies for helping the homeless? It's sort of his thing."

"Oh, is it?" Maddie has asked, instantly curious.

It had taken Liv twice as long to make the short walk to

John's electronics repair shop as usual. She not only didn't have the heart to tell Maddie that the homeless problem couldn't be solved with food, but she also didn't want to rush her on her first excursion through the urban West Coast.

"Of course I can see the chimera," Maddie stated, ruffling the hair on the top of Pickles' head.

"Because it is a glamour that's covering it, right?" Liv asked. "And that doesn't work on giants?"

Maddie nodded.

Of course, neither Rory nor Bermuda had relayed this information to Liv. They liked their little secrets. It made sense now that giants could see past the glamour. However, when the chimera had been locked, no one could see what it truly was.

Pickles began yelping, then jumped off Sophia's lap and threw his paws on Maddie's legs. He transformed into his chimera form, his high-pitched barks becoming loud roars. The giant lion with a serpent's tail and goat's head on his back didn't even knock the giantess over as he jumped on her excitedly.

"She sure is..." John said from the corner of his mouth, giving Liv a meaningful look.

"Animated?" she supplied.

He nodded. "Where did you get her from?"

"Texas," she answered. "Not like the giants we grow here, huh?"

He snorted with laughter. "The Laurenses are just a bit more serious, but yes, Maddie seems great."

The giantess was now holding her chest and nearly buzzing with excitement.

"Maddie, I'm sorry to interrupt, but I want to introduce you to John Carraway. He's one of the Mortal Seven, and this is his chimera," Liv stated, presenting John.

He held his hand out to her, but she didn't take it. Instead, she bowed slightly. "A pleasure to meet you. I suppose you requested my help with the chimera or a House related project?"

Liv shook her head, putting her arm around Sophia as her little sister slipped around her arm, lying her head on her side. She was so much bigger than even the day before. She and the egg were growing at an exponential rate. Sophia already looked eleven, or maybe even twelve. It was too much for Liv, but then she reminded herself that was only a thought and a thought can be changed.

"This is my sister Sophia Beaufont, and she's the reason I requested your help."

Maddie beamed as she looked down at the little girl. "I remember you saying that now. You need help with something for your sister. Pleased to meet you, Sophia Beaufont. And I like your dress."

Sophia curtsied, pulling the skirt of her dress to the side. She was wearing a navy-blue sailor dress that made her appear distinguished and completely adorable at the same time. It was hard for Liv to believe this girl would one day be one of the Dragon Elite. She'd been reading up on the secretive organization, although the only information available on them was considered rumors. According to those, though, the Elite ate raw meat for breakfast, could spear a minotaur with their eyes closed while half-drunk, and were composed entirely of men. Liv wasn't sure how beautiful little Sophia was going to fit in with a group like that, but honestly, she feared more for the Elite than she did for Sophia.

"Thank you," Sophia said to Maddie.

"I asked for your help because we have something very secretive and somewhat delicate we need moved," Liv explained.

The smile dropped from the giantess' face.

"You see, my sister, she—"

"Has magnetized to a dragon egg," Maddie said, cutting Liv off.

"That's right!" Liv exclaimed. "How did you know?"

"I can sense it about her," she explained.

Liv sighed. Giants seemed to know everything. It made her wonder how much Rory didn't tell her, although she'd already guessed it was a great deal.

"Yes, I have a dragon's egg, and we need it transported to someplace safe," Sophia stated. "He doesn't like Liv's place because of all the glamour, and he's gotten too big for us to move easily."

"And you say I'll have help?" Maddie questioned.

"Yes, Rory will be with you. Bermuda and he are at my place going over the plans," Liv stated.

"I'll take you down there," Sophia said, grabbing Maddie's hand and tugging her toward the door.

Liv wouldn't normally allow Sophia to stroll down the block on her own between the shop and the apartment, but she was with a giant. However, Maddie was new to the city.

"Soph," Liv began, a warning in her voice.

"We won't talk to strangers," her sister replied, prompted by her tone.

"And?"

"And we will go straight there and not dawdle," Sophia continued.

"And?" Liv asked again.

"And if any baddies try to stop us, I'll turn them into snails and make us invisible, just in case there are any more of them out there waiting to attack."

Liv smiled. "Good girl."

CHAPTER EIGHT

The pair left the shop, giving Liv a chance to finally look around at the cluttered shelves. A lot of projects had come in recently and were stacking up, but with the egg and the Mortal Seven and everything else, Liv had little time for repairs.

John was just as busy as she was, spying on the Renegades and attending council meetings at the House.

"So, how about I tackle everything on the bottom shelves and you take the stuff I can't reach?" Liv suggested to John, pointing to the shelves up high.

He grinned. "I love your spirit, but I came up with another, better idea."

"Oh?" she questioned as Plato materialized. The lynx gave the chimera a studious glare.

"Well, it was really your idea, but I decided to finally go along with it."

"Yay, you're going to get the council to approve my idea to add an extra hour to every day!" Liv exclaimed.

John shook his head. "No, it appears Father Time has

turned that plan down a few dozen times already. It's out of the council's hands."

Liv thought for a moment. "Oh, then I guess the whole portaling into the past to when the electronics worked isn't going to fly either."

In John's typical easy-going style, he chuckled. "I'm not sure the logistics of that plan add up for me."

"Yeah," Liv stated, searching the shelves.

John picked up a stainless-steel toaster. She thought he was going to inspect it for repair, but instead, he held it, staring at his reflection and fixing his hair—something he never, ever did.

"John, does this plan have anything to do with someone who could actually portal into the past?"

He lowered the toaster. "You mean, Father Time? You're the one who works for him, not me."

"No, I mean—"

The door chimed, and as if cued by the conversation, Alicia De Luca strode into the shop, looking bright and cheerful. She didn't much look like a scientist in her flowing blue sundress and flats, but Liv knew how deceiving appearances could be. This magician was probably one of the most skilled with magical tech of anyone on the planet.

"I knew it! Alicia!" Liv exclaimed, running over and hugging the girl who she'd known as a chicken for the first few weeks they'd been together.

The Italian set down her work bag and gave Liv a tight hug, smiling at her when she pulled away. Her long brown hair was piled on her head in a French twist, and around her neck was a small charm of a chicken.

Liv pointed at the jewelry. "I like it."

Alicia touched her hand softly to her chest. "I think some might want to forget being stuck as a chicken, but I try to think of it in terms of the positives. If that hadn't happened, I would never have met you. My shop is prospering more than ever. The House has me working on special contracts for them." Her eyes flickered to John. "And of course, I met Mr. Carraway."

As if Liv didn't exist anymore, the scientist strode past her, marching in John's direction. She threw her arms around him, squealing slightly when he picked her up and twirled her.

Pickles, still in chimera form, pressed in close to the pair as if hoping to join in the embrace.

Alicia glanced over her shoulder at the chimera, finally pulling away from John. "Oh, and you, Pickles. I've heard all about how amazing you are, and now I get to see for myself." Not like petting a dog on the head, but as if greeting a majestic being, Alicia offered her hand for the chimera to inspect. He sniffed it once, pressing his nose affectionately into it. Realizing she'd been given permission, Alicia ran her fingers over the top of the chimera's head.

"Aw, isn't that the sweetest thing you've ever seen?" Liv asked Plato, who had jumped up on the workstation beside her.

He shook his head, not appearing impressed.

"If you don't think so, all you have to do is say so," Liv urged.

Plato remained silent.

Alicia pulled her hand away from Pickles and glanced at

John. "Mortal Seven. It's simply wonderful." Her Italian accent made every word sound like music.

"He's even more handsome than before, huh?" Liv said, making John blush furiously.

"I didn't think it possible," Alicia agreed, all unabashed affection for the man before her. She glanced around the shop. "You're weren't kidding, John. Your projects really are piling up."

"You called Alicia to help? I knew it! It was a great idea I had," Liv exclaimed.

He nodded proudly. "And even though she's got her own shop and contracts with the House, she agreed."

Alicia picked up her bag and began rummaging through it. "Oh, don't be silly. My shop can pretty much run itself since I've got my assistants to help."

"You mean Laidback Lion and Plotting Panda?" Liv asked, referring to the robots Alicia had built, which were enhanced with amazing magical tech, making them intuitive and creative.

"Yes, and I gave them both upgrades," Alicia stated. "Now they are big enough to handle the day-to-day operations of the shop. I'll just pop over every other day to see if there's anything they need, which means I can help out here with repairs while also working on House contracts."

"Wow, you're a lifesaver," Liv said, letting out a breath of relief.

Alicia laughed. "Says the girl who actually saved my life."

"I can help with a few projects before tonight's Council meeting, but Liv needs to be off," John said, and Liv could have sworn she was being dismissed.

"Yes, that's right. I have to go now. There's a giant, a tiny magician, and an ungrateful houseguest I need to meet up with." Liv started for the front door, noticing someone approaching quickly from the other side. She titled her head, trying to make out the figure through the blurry glass.

Chloe threw open the door just as Liv stepped back, her hand automatically going to Bellator.

"Jonathon Carraway!" Chloe yelled, not even seeming to notice Liv as she marched through the door and straight over to John. "You are dead meat!"

CHAPTER NINE

"Who's Jonathon?" Liv asked, looking down at Plato. He shrugged as if he had no clue.

"Chloe?" John asked. "What are you doing here?"

"What am I doing here?" Chloe glanced at Alicia, giving her a cold stare before returning her gaze to John, who seemed unflustered. "I have urgent business to discuss with you."

"Go on, then," John urged.

The magician's hair was windswept, and her cheeks were red like she'd run a mile in her knee-high boots to get there. Liv paused by the door, not in a hurry to leave there now. John had been leading Chloe on, secretly funneling information she told him about the Renegades to Liv and the council while giving the wicked magician wrong information about the House of Fourteen.

"I need to speak to you alone!" Chloe yelled, her eyes bulging.

Pickles, still in chimera form, sunk down, growling at the woman.

"I'm afraid I'm in the middle of something, Chloe," John stated, his tone even. "Can you just give me a minute? This is my new—"

"I don't care who this hussy is," Chloe stated, cutting him off.

"Actually, she's not a—"

"John, that thing I told you about? Well, I have reason to believe you've leaked the information," Chloe said, stabbing a finger into his chest and pressing him back an inch.

Pickles growled deeper, about to lunge for the magician.

To Liv's surprise, John actually held up a hand, stopping his chimera from defending him. "It's okay, boy. I've got this." He turned his attention to Chloe, who was trying to bear down on him with intimidation. "I assure you I didn't tell anyone about Sid and his...establishment."

"Then why was he raided by the House and shut down?" Chloe asked, narrowing her eyes at him.

John scratched his head, seemingly thoroughly perplexed. "Well, I haven't got a clue, darling. I really wish I did."

Chloe threw her hands in the air before turning and marching around the shop. Alicia watched, not at all put off by the angry woman's display. "And none of the information you've given me about the House has panned out." She stopped and tilted her head to the side, giving John a scrutinizing glare. "It's almost as if..."

"John doesn't know a thing about the House," Liv supplied.

Chloe spun, seeming to notice Liv for the first time.

"Why is your assistant always butting her nose in where it doesn't belong?"

"I was never taught any better," Liv stated. "And I don't know much about this House stuff, but John is fairly new to it. It's pretty naïve to think he'd offer you anything of use."

Chloe didn't think Liv was a threat. That had been clear since the beginning. She merely thought she was a simple magician who worked in his shop. It appeared she'd made the same assumption about Alicia. The thing about people who were driven by ego was they usually inflated their own self-worth so much that they discounted that of others, which was a huge mistake. One Liv hoped to capitalize upon.

"Keep your mouth shut, apprentice," Chloe fired at Liv. "Grownups are having a conversation."

"Sorry, I'll just go back to doing my finger paints and eating my animal crackers," Liv said, catching a weird glint in Alicia's eyes. The scientist had something in her hands that she was hiding.

Chloe rounded on John, coming at him again. "If I find out you have been holding out on me, I'll have every hair on your head. Do you understand?"

Pickles appeared to be about to pounce on the bold magician. However, Alicia held her hand out to the chimera, pausing him. She reached out, lightly touching Chloe on the shoulder. *"Mi scusi, ma sei una vera stronza."*

Chloe spun to face Alicia. "What? What did you say to me? And who are you?"

Liv kept her laugh locked in her mouth. "This is Alic—"

"Stop talking to me, apprentice!" Chloe yelled, shaking

her head at Alicia. "And you as well, foreigner. I'm here to speak to John."

"*Molto bene si strega ripugnante*," Alicia said, backing up and throwing her hands in the air.

Chloe shook her head. "Whatever. John, you should really have people who speak English working for you."

John, who also knew, even with his limited understanding of the Italian language, that Alicia had insulted Chloe, simply shrugged.

Chloe backed away, shaking her head at him. "I thought you and I could actually help each other, but now I see you're as useless as you were before. Nothing has changed. Good riddance, John."

With that, Chloe stormed out of the electronics repair shop.

The air seemed to change as soon as the vixen was gone. John sighed with relief, putting his hand on Pickles' head as if for support.

"Sorry, Liv, I think I just blew my chance of helping the House with the Renegades," he said somberly.

She shook her head. "Hey, we brought down Sid Encore and his horrid amusement park. Oh, and freed a few dozen unicorns. I'd call that a win."

Alicia smiled, her brown eyes lighting up. "I wouldn't despair just yet, John." She held up a small remote she'd pulled from her bag.

"Because you've got a remote control car you're going to allow us to play with?" Liv asked, strangely excited about the prospect.

Alicia laughed. "No, because I've placed a tracker on that awful woman's jacket. It will bury itself in the fabric, going completely unnoticed, and it's impervious to the elements. Even if she won't give John any more information, she's sure to lead us to a place of importance sooner or later."

Liv rejoiced, jumping up and down. "Like the headquarters of the Renegades!"

John's mouth fell open. "A place she wouldn't even mention to me before. She only mentioned Sid in passing. This is real progress, Alicia."

The scientist beamed. "I'd say it was a team effort. And now you don't have to endure any more time with that—"

"'Bitch' is the name I think you called her," Liv said, finishing her sentence.

"And also something about a horrid witch," John said with a laugh. "I'm not sure if that's a criticism of magicians or not."

"It's not," Liv assured him. "Witches don't exist. But if they did, Chloe would definitely be a horrid one."

"And one you don't have to risk being around anymore," Alicia stated with relief. Yes, she was probably worried about John's safety around a loose cannon like Chloe, but she also seemed relieved that John wouldn't have to spend any more time with his ex-wife.

If at all possible, Liv liked Alicia De Luca even more now.

CHAPTER TEN

Rory paused outside the open door of Liv's apartment like he all of a sudden needed an invitation to come in.

Liv was sampling the pastries Clark had been making when she noticed the giant standing awkwardly in the doorway. She slid into view in the hallway with her arms crossed. "What are you doing?"

He jumped at the sight of her. "I'm just waiting for Mum. She insisted on parking the moving truck."

"Even though you're the one who has to drive it?" Liv asked.

His eyes slid to the right, his lips pressing into a hard line.

"So, about this secret job of yours that isn't so secret," Liv began. "We haven't had a good chance to discuss it yet."

"Do we really have to do this now?" Rory asked, looking over Liv's shoulder expectantly.

"If not now, when, Rory Laurens?" she questioned. "I

mean, you think you know someone, even though they keep tons of secrets and refuse to tell you what they do for a living, and then you find out that they are an accountant."

"If Mum hears you talking about the family business, she'll—"

"What?" Liv cut him off. "Severely disapprove of me? Tell me I'm uncouth? Complain about my sarcastic nature? Oh, no! And that would be different from any other interaction with Mrs. Laurens how?"

Clark came up next to Liv holding a tray of stuffed mushrooms. "Here, Rory. I tried the recipe you gave me. It makes the mushrooms the perfect consistency. Not too soft or chewy. Try them."

Rory gave him a polite smile as he took one of the mushrooms. He popped it into his mouth and nodded. "Very good."

"I'll see if Sophia and Matilda want to try one," Clark said, trotting for the back.

Rory appeared to have swallowed the mushroom without chewing all of a sudden. Liv pretended not to notice this as she rocked forward on her toes and back again. "Did you know there are three different types of accountants?"

Rory's eyes fluttered with annoyance.

"Yep," Liv continued. "There are those who can count and those who can't."

The giant sighed.

"Okay, fine. I'm still working on the jokes," Liv stated. "So, all the hobbies were your outlet to get away from the boring accounting business, which you're required to do because Mum says so, right? Why don't you just tell your mum that it drains your soul and do what you really want to?" Liv paused and thought for a moment. "Wait, what *do* you really want to do?"

He shook his head. "I'm not telling you."

"Typical."

"You'll just make fun of me and think it's silly," he added.

Liv stuck her hands on her hips. "When have I, Rory Jordan Laurens, ever made fun of you?"

"That's not my middle name," he stated.

She scoffed. "I know that, Rory Marcus Laurens."

"Okay, we have fifteen minutes until we have to move the truck," Bermuda said, breathing with great difficulty as she lumbered up the stairs. "We're in a loading zone."

Liv smiled at the giantess, who didn't return it. "You do realize we are magical creatures who can just magic our way around parking rules and regulations, right?"

Bermuda pulled the bonnet she was wearing off her head. She looked like she was ready for Sunday brunch in her usual floral dress and gaudy jewelry. "Really, Warrior Beaufont. Does the House know you go around abusing your magical powers?"

"They encourage it since my quests save the mortal world and preserve the lives of magical creatures," Liv refuted.

Bermuda pulled off her gloves, dismissing Liv as she strode past her. "Really, you can't always legitimize your bad behavior with those excuses."

Liv gave Rory a commiserating expression, which he didn't return.

"So, the giant you got to help us," Bermuda said, laying

her handbag on the table, her eyes lingering on the dust on it for a moment. "Is it Zed who works at the zoo in San Diego?"

"No, actually—"

"Yes, he'd be at the festivities on the island, wouldn't he," Bermuda said, cutting Liv off. "Oh, it must be one of the Simpson brothers. They usually have to stick around since the ferries to Catalina Island run consistently this time of year."

"Actually, remember that favor Liam Goldwater owes you?" Liv said, sliding behind Rory for protection.

Bermuda spun, her face flushing red. "Liam! In Texas! The one who runs the barbeque restaurant? Are you telling me you got him to help?"

Matilda Goldwater strode out of the hallway, giving Sophia a piggyback ride. Bermuda looked like she was going to faint when she caught sight of the giantess.

"Surprise," Liv said, only her head peeking around Rory.

"Matilda Goldwater? Is that really you?" Bermuda questioned. "Well, I haven't seen you since you were yay-high to my hip."

"Which, incidentally, is how tall I am currently," Liv said in a hushed voice to Rory. He didn't laugh, probably because he didn't hear her, even though she was right behind him. His eyes were centered on the giantess who was carefully sliding Sophia to the ground.

"Mrs. Laurens," Matilda said, bowing. "It's wonderful to see you again."

Bermuda didn't reply. Instead, she turned to where Liv

was hiding. "Did you say something about the favor Liam owes me?"

"I did," Liv said ducking out from behind Rory, but only slightly. "Looks like everything is even between you and him for whatever happened at the Rock of Gibraltar."

"I saved the lives of everyone in his village," Bermuda stated. "That was before Matilda and the restaurant, but really, Warrior Beaufont."

Liv decided to act like an adult and stepped out from behind Rory. "And now we have the help we'll need to get the egg to safety, which is what's important, right?"

Bermuda lowered her chin and gave Liv a murderous glare.

She cupped her ear. "What? Oh, I think I hear Alfred calling you, Sophia." Liv bolted forward, grabbing her little sister by the hand and dragged her back down the hallway. "We're just going to give the dragon and its rider a chance to say goodbye. Won't be long. Then we'll be off."

"She's going to kill you, isn't she?" Sophia asked when Liv had finally released her.

Liv shook her head. "No, but I do have to ride with her on this voyage to transport the egg, and I'm certain she's going to be rather hostile. It's fine. We're taking the 405, so everyone in traffic will be hostile."

Sophia smiled, but it was completely forced. Her eyes swiveled to the shimmering blue egg next to her bed.

"Hey," Liv said, realizing what was going on. "It's not forever, and you get to go over there and visit him."

Sophia nodded. "I know. I've just gotten so used to having him beside me all the time."

Liv stooped down and peered up at her little sister. "And for the rest of your lives, you and Frank will be together."

This seemed to make the little magician feel slightly better.

"But I know how you feel," Liv stated. "Plato is like my familiar. He's a part of me, and when he's not around, sometimes it feels like I'm lost."

"Where is he now?" Sophia asked.

Liv didn't even hesitate. "He's standing in the doorway at my back."

Sophia's eyes darted to the side, awe covering her face. "How did you know?"

Liv smiled. "I just did. That's the thing; when you're bonded to someone, whether a dragon or a lynx or your amazing little sister, you just know things about them. Kind of like I know you're going to go on to do incredible things. But first, we need to keep you safe and give you some time to grow up a little. I think that it's what Mom and Dad would have wanted."

Sophia nodded at once. "I think so too, and I have the rest of my life for adventures. But no matter what, Liv, no matter what happens when my dragon hatches, I'll always be here for you and Clark."

It felt so strange to Liv that her little sister was somehow consoling her, being careful with her feelings.

"Soph, once that dragon hatches, your life is going to take you in new directions," Liv stated. "You'll go places where we can't follow you. And although we will do whatever we can to help and protect you, it's unwise to think we will always be together."

Sophia grabbed Liv with an intensity that made her gasp. Her little arms were strong as she tugged her sister into her. "I know we will, Liv, because no matter what, *familia est sempiternum.*"

CHAPTER ELEVEN

With an obvious overabundance of nervous tension, Bermuda Laurens tapped the steering wheel of the truck she was driving. Liv had offered to drive, but the giantess explained that she was an expert getaway driver.

"What are we getting away from?" Liv asked. "I thought we were following Rory and Maddie with the egg."

"Poachers will try all sorts of tactics to get to the egg," Bermuda had stated, turning the radio to a classical station. "We're going to have to run interference."

Apparently, the poachers would be alerted that a very valuable magical object was being transported as soon as it left Liv's place on the truck. Once it was at Rory's, there were force fields that would shield it again. The twenty-minute commute, which could be over two hours in traffic, was their chance to steal the egg. Liv didn't know how they'd do that since she'd watched Rory and Maddie struggle for half an hour to load the egg into the back of the truck. However, Bermuda had stated that they were using great care, and poachers didn't have the same considerations.

"So, how great were those stuffed mushrooms Clark—"

"You shouldn't have brought her here," Bermuda said, cutting Liv off, her gloved hands tight on the steering wheel.

Liv knew exactly who the "her" was that she was referring too, but she thought it would be more fun if she acted as if she didn't. "Oh, well, Sophia wanted to live with me, and I—"

"I'm talking about Matilda Goldwater," Bermuda stated tersely, following the moving truck as it sped onto the highway.

"I know you think I hang out with giants all the time, but it may surprise you to find out that you and Rory are the only ones."

Bermuda cast a disapproving look at her. "Are you tall enough to be sitting in the front seat?"

Liv wanted to laugh. That almost sounded like a joke. "Well, I didn't bring my booster seat, but I thought that if I flew forward, you'd throw a protective arm in front of me."

"I won't," Bermuda stated matter-of-factly.

"Namaste to you, too."

"And really, of all the giants you could have recruited, you had to go and pick—"

"What, a Goldwater?" Liv asked. "I'm sorry about the favor thing. Liam gave me an in, and I took it. He seemed to think very fondly of you."

"Of course, he does," Bermuda stated, following every single traffic law down to the letter as she merged onto the congested freeway. "I saved his entire village."

Liv leaned forward, watching as a vehicle tried to speed ahead and cut them off, taking the spot between them and the moving truck Rory was driving. "You may want to—"

"Don't tell me how to drive," Bermuda stated. "And no, it's not that she's a Goldwater. It's that she's—"

"A Texan?" Liv supplied. "I know, I know. They are very prideful people, but I think most of them are sweethearts if you can get over the fact that they talk slow and make their tea overly sweet."

"No, Warrior Beaufont, I mean the fact that she's…well, a she."

"Oh," Liv said, wondering why it hadn't dawned on her before. The sedan succeeded in cutting between them and the moving truck. "So these poachers. Could they be in unsuspecting vehicles, like that one?"

Bermuda shook her head. "No, those are just inconsiderate jerks. Poachers will fly in and try to storm the truck."

"Like on brooms?" Liv asked.

The giantess rolled her eyes. "No, not on…oh, that was one of those jokes, wasn't it?"

"It obviously wasn't a very good one," Liv admitted. "I'm just wondering what I'm looking for."

Traffic was suddenly at a standstill. That didn't give Liv any confidence. She liked it better when they were moving. It felt like progress.

"Just keep your eye out for anything suspicious," Bermuda stated. "I'm used to tracking those guys, so I'll recognize them when they show up. Then I'm going to want you to employ your combat magic."

Liv flexed her pointer finger. "I can do that. I've been

practicing blasting the mustard off of a hotdog. My aim is really good."

Bermuda shot her a look of disapproval. "Only take a shot if the poacher is far from the truck. We can't take any chances."

"You get that I do this kind of stuff for a living?" Liv stated. "Speaking of which, Rory is an accountant, huh?"

"Yes," Bermuda stated, sitting up taller. "Laurens Accounting has been in the family for generations."

"Really? I would have thought that on the island you wouldn't need accounting. How hard is it to divide up rocks among..." Liv's voice trailed away, encouraged to stop talking by the murderous look on Bermuda's face.

"I'll have you know that accounting is one of the oldest professions."

"About like prostitution," Liv added.

"No, not like...anyway, we are very proud of our business. Rory is quite good at it."

"But does he like it?" Liv asked.

Bermuda opened her mouth to answer but stalled. "Well, of course, he does. What's not to like?"

"Are you a part of the business?" Liv questioned.

"Of course not. You know very well that I'm an explorer. I chronicle magical creatures and plants and other things."

"Oh, because that's your passion," Liv stated.

"Yes, because it's my passion."

"But Rory doesn't get to follow his passion," Liv kept going.

"Well, it's not that. He loves accounting."

"Does he?" Liv questioned. She knew she might be

overstepping her boundaries. Rory could hate her for it. But she'd rather that than her friend continue to do something he didn't enjoy because his mother intimidated every living soul on the planet. Well, not her, but that was because she'd met the most soulless creatures.

"Yes, I know for a fact that Rory loves accounting," Bermuda stated.

"Because he's told you this?"

"Warrior Beaufont, where are you going with this?"

Liv took a deep breath. Sat up straighter. Turned to face the giantess whose head was rubbing the ceiling of the truck she was driving. "Mrs. Laurens, I respect you a great deal, but you don't accept people for who they are. Instead, you cast judgments, criticize, and try to make us all conform to what you want us to be. I wonder if, for just one moment, you could simply look at the people in your life through the same lens that you do the creatures you chronicle. Simply appreciate who they are with unyielding understanding for their uniqueness.

"I think you'd find you'd understand those around you with the same grace and beauty as the ones you've written about in your books, which are famous for a reason. You have a wonderful perspective, but only when you're not—"

"Shush!" Bermuda yelled, making Liv tense. She'd gone too far. She was surprised the giantess had allowed her to talk that long and say that much.

"I'm sorry if I overstepped my boundaries," Liv said.

"You did," Bermuda stated at once. "But we will discuss that later. For now, we have poachers to attend to."

She pointed out the window to where a bird was flapping its wings, soaring only feet above the stalled truck.

"Let me guess," Liv began. "That's not a bird, is it?"

Bermuda shook her head, looking around at the other cars, also not moving in traffic.

"It's something that's glamoured, isn't it?" Liv dared to guess.

"Yes," Bermuda answered.

Liv opened the car door and stepped out onto the pavement.

"What are you doing?" Bermuda asked.

Liv ducked back through the open window. "Doing what I came here for. You spot the poachers, and I make them pay."

CHAPTER TWELVE

Once out of the vehicle, Liv felt strange standing around a bunch of idling cars on the freeway. Many of the drivers gave her cautious glances, as if worried she was a road-raging passenger about to go crazy from sitting in traffic.

If they think I'm crazy now, just wait, Liv thought, pointing her finger at the hawk circling above the moving truck. She wasn't sure what the bird actually was. It could have been a person or a helicopter glamoured to look like something inconspicuous. There was only one way to find out, and that was to knock it down.

A blast of green light shot from the end of Liv's finger, narrowly missing the hawk, which squawked its disapproval when one of its wings was almost hit. She tried again, but whatever it was was fast, darting away from her attacks.

"Hey! Don't mess with that bird!" a guy yelled from his open car window.

"I'm a Warrior for the House of Fourteen!" Liv exclaimed, trying to anticipate which way the bird was going to fly so she could cut it off.

"I don't care who you're with," someone else yelled. "We don't hurt animals."

Ironically, these mortals didn't realize that was exactly what Liv was trying to do: protect an animal from harm. She sort of missed the days when mortals couldn't see magic. Back then, they would have just seen Liv pointing into the sky or something else of little interest or concern.

Liv shot more bolts in quick succession, none of them hitting the bird-thing.

"Hey, lady!" the guy yelled again. "Leave the bird alone, or I'll have to stop you."

Liv spun around. "Look, I'm a police officer, in a way, for a magical organization. Stop me, and you're going to be sorry."

"Where's your badge?"

Liv grunted. She needed a freaking badge.

"Warrior Beaufont!" Bermuda called, urgency in her voice.

Liv turned just in time to see the bird diving toward the truck. That didn't look good. With a quick and focused effort, she sent another attack at the fast-moving object. It froze in mid-air, shifting several times before it took the form of a woman with green hair and a staff, wearing a cape and billowing pants.

"Whoa!" one of the men hanging out of the car windows exclaimed as the figure rolled onto the roof of the truck.

"I told you!" Liv called to them arrogantly, sprinting for

the side of the truck. She climbed up, giving Maddie a reassuring look in the side mirror. "Don't worry. I've got this."

The giantess nodded although she didn't appear totally reassured.

When Liv's hand reached the top of the truck, a firm boot crashed down on it, and it made a loud popping sound. She wailed from the excruciating pain of having her finger broken. Her head whipped up to see a woman with a vengeful grimace staring down at her.

The woman brought her boot up and back like she was about to kick Liv in the face. Even though her finger was sticking out at a weird angle, she could still use the hand. She reached out just before the foot connected with her face, grabbing the woman's billowing pants and yanking her forward, sending her to her back on the roof of the truck.

Seizing her opportunity, Liv jumped up onto the truck, shaking her hand like that might help her finger. It didn't. She pulled Bellator and let it lead the way, striking at the woman. She rolled to the side, evading the attack. Bellator struck into the top of the truck.

Looked like they weren't getting their deposit back on the rental truck, Liv thought, working to pull the sword out.

"Wow!" someone yelled from the cars. "They are fighting!"

The poacher popped to her feet like Akio did in training, ricocheting off her back. Liv yanked Bellator free just in time and swung it. The woman hopped back, sucking in her stomach to avoid getting sliced.

Rory slapped the roof. "We're moving!"

Liv nearly lost her balance as the truck started to accelerate. *Oh, great. Crazy. I get to fight a deranged poacher on top of a moving vehicle.*

The woman held her staff to the side, parrying the attacks Liv threw at her one after the other.

She couldn't look away long enough to see what Bermuda was saying or indicating, but the giantess one car back was definitely trying to communicate something. She shook her head radically at her, hoping she got the point.

The poacher swiped her staff hard against Bellator while putting her foot behind Liv's and tripping her, knocking her back. The wind flew out of her lungs as her head hung over the side of the truck. She'd definitely need a massage after this.

The only thing lucky about the position she was in right then was that Bermuda had switched lanes and pulled up beside the truck. She yelled something through the open car window. It sounded like, "Do you want a ride?"

Liv shook her head, rolling to the side as the crazed poacher used her staff like a hammer. When the woman was bent over, having missed, Liv swung Bellator over in an arc, slicing the staff in two. A jolt of magic shot from the staff, throwing the woman off the top of the truck and sending her into the windshield of the sedan behind them.

Liv grimaced at the sight. It wasn't bloody, since the poacher was pretty tough. She was already shaking her head from the assault like it had merely dazed her. The driver ducked his head out the window, a look of shock on his face.

"Try using your windshield wipers to get her off," Liv called. "That should help."

"Warrior Beaufont!" Bermuda called from the car speeding beside her. They were picking up speed now.

Great, the 405 is finally moving, and I'm on top of a truck.

"What?" Liv yelled at Bermuda.

"On the other side!"

Liv's eyes widened as the implications sank in. She darted to the far side of the truck, nearly losing her balance. To her horror, a magician was standing on the back bumper, sawing a large hole in the side of the vehicle with magic.

"Oh, hell, nah!" Liv said, sheathing Bellator and sending a fireball at the man.

He looked up just as the blast connected with his midsection, knocking him into the road. The car behind them, where the woman had landed and strangely disappeared, nearly ran over the man but swerved at the last moment, causing a ripple of collisions behind them. Liv looked out from the top of the truck, realizing that the 405 was going to be backed up for hours due to this snafu. She turned back, looking ahead, grateful the road was now clear.

A sudden scream accosted Liv's attention. She turned, finding Bermuda waving her hands wildly from the speeding car.

"What?" Liv called.

Bermuda pointed behind the truck. Many of the vehicles had unfortunately been involved in one of the collisions that were a result of this mayhem. There were a few that were still keeping pace with traffic, though.

"The car!" Bermuda yelled clear and loud so Liv could make out her words.

Liv pointed, her hair whipping her in the face as she stood on top of the moving truck.

"That car?" she asked, pointing at the one in the lane behind Bermuda.

She shook her head.

Liv pointed to the one with the man who had been angered about her trying to harm a defenseless bird. "That one?"

Again the giantess shook her head.

Liv was about to guess again when the sedan that had been hit by the woman with green hair speed up, slamming into the back of the truck and making Liv tumble forward. She fell over the side of the truck but was able to grab onto the back even though her finger was screaming from the pain of being broken.

Bermuda slowed enough to catch sight of Liv dangling over the side, relief on her face when she saw that she hadn't fallen to the road and been run over.

"Oh, that car," Liv said, trying to hike her feet up over the top again.

Another assault on the truck nearly sent her flying off. The bumper of the car almost rammed into Liv's feet, which were flailing every which way. A car shouldn't have had such an impact on a sturdy moving truck, which meant it wasn't a normal car.

"The car is enhanced!" Bermuda yelled, driving beside Liv, who was still hanging off the side of the truck.

"Thanks," Liv said dryly.

"Don't hit it with anything!" Bermuda yelled.

"Cool. I'll just politely tell them to stop!" Liv screamed back, the wind still assaulting her face.

"The outside of the car is protected from damage," Bermuda stated. "Look!" She pointed at the car, which seemed like it was about to make another crash attempt.

Liv sucked in a quick breath and slid down the side, holding onto the corner of the truck with all her might as the car rammed them again. This time Rory had anticipated it and sped up so it was only a minor scrape. However, Liv had a chance to see what Bermuda meant. The car's windshield which should have been cracked and severely damaged from the poacher blasting into it, but it was completely unharmed.

"Well, hell!" Liv yelled. "What am I going to do?"

If she couldn't send fireballs or a huge gale at the car, how was she going to stop it?

"Here!" Bermuda said and tossed something at her through the open car window.

To Liv's surprise, she was able to catch the object. It was a tiny perfume bottle.

"Thanks, but I was just going to shower later!" Liv said, grimacing in frustration at the giantess speeding along beside her.

"Attack from the inside," Bermuda stated, indicating the car, which looked ready to make another attempt.

Liv didn't know what she was referring to until she noticed that the windows of the car were down. That was helpful. However, what wasn't at all good was that the passengers were now all hanging out the sides, many of them pointing in Liv's direction.

In unison, they all fired at the wheels of the truck. Liv held on for dear life, waiting for the truck to careen to the side with flat tires. However, a barrier shot up between the truck and the car. Liv turned and saw Bermuda holding up a protective hand. She was providing a shield, but as with all protective spells, it wouldn't last long.

Liv was just about to make her move when the truck changed lanes suddenly, taking an exit as if Rory had just remembered where he lived.

Many of the vehicles he cut off honked, like they were put out that the moving truck with a hole in the side and a magician hanging off it had been rude to not use a blinker before exiting.

The car sped after them, the magicians continuing to fire and quickly burning through the shield. One more blast and it would be down, which meant Liv had to act before it was too late. These poachers seemed bent on destroying the truck if they couldn't have its contents.

She slammed into the truck, her face taking the brunt of the impact as it came to a swift halt at a stoplight. The magicians sped after them, veering around cars to catch up. They were one car behind them. Bermuda was stuck at the back of the line of exiting cars. Liv peered around the side of the truck, trying to gauge the best time for her next trick. The light turned green.

She turned around, holding onto the side, and with a swift movement of her hand, she pushed the car just between the truck and the poachers to the side, easily putting it onto the shoulder. The driver gawked, looking at the dashboard of the car like there was a reason for the sudden strange behavior of the vehicle.

The poachers sped forward just as Rory accelerated, whipping the truck to the side as he quickly turned. Liv closed her eyes, made a silent prayer, and then leapt off the moving truck. She felt the rough assault of the car as she crashed into it.

Her eyes whipped open, and she looked through the windshield at the jerks who had been chasing them. Three magicians with sullen faces.

They yelled! One of them began to climb out the window. Liv pushed her feet under her, but they slipped out several times, making her chin hit the car as it accelerated. She finally got moving, but the magician who was hanging out the passenger side was shooting spells at her.

Holding onto the side of the car, she swung her legs around, taking her body completely sideways and kicking the guy in the face. His hand flew to his face as he sank back down. From the backseat, on the other side, the third guy started to crawl out.

They were on a straightaway, quickly gaining speed, but also getting closer to Rory's house. They needed to get the egg to safety. Also, they needed to get rid of these guys before they got any closer. The less they knew about the safe location, the better.

Liv had a choice. She could stop the guy crawling out of the vehicle, or she could stop the car. She glanced up. Bermuda was quickly swerving around traffic, making up for lost time.

Liv yanked the perfume bottle up. Holding on with one hand, she pulled the cork out with her teeth. Then she swung over the side, her face upside down as she looked through the back window.

"Hey, boys!" she called.

The one trying to get out ducked back in. The driver turned around, batting at her. The one she had kicked in the face was nursing a broken nose.

"Just so you know," Liv continued, "you all stink." She tossed the bottle into the car and then threw herself back. Not hesitating, she jumped to her feet and threw herself off the back of the vehicle, leaping through the air.

Bermuda was too far away. She'd never make it.

The giantess, sensing the fatal problem, gunned it. Liv's arms and legs circled several times in what felt like slow motion—and then she landed on the hood of Bermuda's truck with a thud.

"Hi!" Liv squeaked, seeing Bermuda through the window.

Like a child out after curfew, Bermuda waved her in. "Would you get in here already?"

Liv laughed as she dove around the side of the windshield and in through the open window.

She slid into her seat as something inside the car in front of them exploded, green smoke filling the compartment. It rammed into the median and crashed into a sign, where it halted. As they drove past, Liv noticed three passed-out figures, their head all lolling to the side. They weren't going anywhere for a while.

Bermuda swerved around the corner and slowed the car casually, like they had just taken a leisurely Sunday drive. "Well, I guess that was okay."

Liv glanced at the giantess, slightly annoyed, her hand throbbing and her face bruised. "Yeah, it was totally okay."

Bermuda sighed as she pulled the car into the driveway of Rory's house just behind the moving truck.

"Oh, we're already here?" Liv complained, looking around. "I was hoping we could stop at a drive-through for curly fries."

CHAPTER THIRTEEN

"Breaker, breaker one-nine," Liv said into the phone. "This is Bellator's Mom, looking for Demon Slayer."

"Liv, the caller ID says it's you," Stefan stated. "You looking for me?"

"Yeah, I've just always wanted to say that on the phone," she said, earning a rude stare from Bermuda. "Will you come over to Rory's? I've got some scum I need you to take into the House of Fourteen before the mortal authorities get to them."

"Sure thing," Stefan said. "I'll portal over if you send me their exact location."

"Already done. I want you to stick them in the dungeon and forget to file a report."

"But they'll rot down there," Stefan stated.

"Yeah, exactly. They are a bunch of poachers."

"Say no more, darling."

Liv hung up the phone, grateful to have someone she could rely on so heavily. She didn't even mind that he'd called her darling, although she might punch him in the shoulder for it later...lightly.

"Well, we did our part!" Liv held up a hand, offering Bermuda a high five. The giantess simply shook her head at her.

"Don't think I forgot what you were saying earlier," she said, watching as Rory and Maddie unloaded the truck, taking great care with the massive egg.

"About wanting curly fries?" Liv said, hope in her voice. "Yeah, I think if you go down that way, there's a good diner."

Bermuda shook her head, pulling her hat from the back and sticking it on her head. "No, about how I need to accept the people in my life."

"Well, it wasn't one of my best speeches, but I'm grateful it resonated with you," Liv said, getting out the car and remembering that one of her fingers was broken. She immediately cradled it to her chest.

For a giantess, Bermuda was pretty fast at running around the vehicle and taking a position right in front of Liv. "I don't think you're right."

"About which part?" Liv asked, the pain distracting her a great deal.

"I'm very accepting of you and others."

"And you never tell us how to live our lives?" Liv questioned. "Or pass judgment on us for not meeting your expectations?"

Bermuda harrumphed. "When you've seen as many things as I have, you simply know how things should be."

"But shouldn't we all be allowed to live our lives the way we want?" Liv questioned, pointing as Rory smirked when Maddie tried to push his hair out of his face as he held onto the egg with both hands. "Maybe make friends with the people we like, and do that which makes our soul sing?"

Bermuda's face flushed red. "No!"

Rory and Maddie whipped their heads around, sudden worry on their face.

Liv held up her hand. "I asked Mrs. Laurens if she'd fix my finger, but apparently medical magic isn't something she feels comfortable with. And I'm not really feeling up for the job. I'm afraid I'll mess it up more. Rory, do you have any whiskey?"

He nodded, turning for the back gate and lumbering forward with the egg.

Bermuda gave Liv a punishing glare. "If I didn't know any better, I would think you're intervening between Rory and me, Warrior Beaufont."

Liv strode after Rory, turning around to face Bermuda as she walked backward. "And if I didn't know any better, I would think deep down, you know I'm right too."

"Why is that?"

"Because a woman like you, who has cataloged almost every magical species on the planet, has to know when nature needs to run its course," Liv reasoned. "Sometimes you have to allow others to be who they are. Otherwise, they won't flourish."

CHAPTER FOURTEEN

Once Liv had confirmed that the dragon's egg was secure and Bermuda wasn't close to killing her, she decided to take her leave. The giantess probably would have let everything she'd said go, but then Liv had really overstepped her boundaries and offered up the idea that Maddie should stay with Rory for a bit. The Texan wanted to see more of the West Coast, but the best excuse Bermuda couldn't refute was that having more giants' magical energy around the egg would help shield it from the Dragon Elite.

Reluctantly, and with a death stare focused in Liv's direction, Rory's mum had agreed. Liv was pretty sure Bermuda hadn't gotten over her attempt at intervening. She wasn't worried, though. Bermuda Laurens was tough, but something in the sturdy woman looked close to breaking. Maybe because as Liv was leaving, she'd stopped her to say, "You weren't horrible with the poachers."

"Thanks," Liv said, offering a polite smile and trying to get out the door. The sooner she got to the House, the sooner Hester DeVries could fix her finger, which was throbbing horribly.

"What I meant to say is, I've heard about some of the brave acts you've done," Bermuda went on, pushing the door closed as Liv tried to leave. "However, seeing them today in person was quite different."

Liv tilted her head to the side, intrigued. "Are you saying you were impressed by me?"

"Putting words in my mouth is never wise, Warrior Beaufont."

Liv nodded. "Well, I appreciate your words of appreciation, which is how I interpret them. Excuse me if that's wrong."

Bermuda then glanced at the kitchen, where Maddie was teaching Rory how to make the Goldwaters' secret recipe for barbeque sauce. The giggling was obviously interrupting Bermuda's train of thought. "Anyway, I'll take what you said about my son and others I judge under consideration, and in the meantime, I just want you to know that you're a brave magician."

Liv thought that was the end of it. She opened her mouth to thank Bermuda, but the giantess held up her hand, pausing her.

"There's more," Bermuda stated, reluctance in her voice. "Warriors have to be brave. It's part of the oath you take for the House of Fourteen, although I've witnessed many break it. However, today, what you did was as a sister. You risked your life to protect something that means a lot to Sophia, although we both know it will inevitably take her away from you. Still, you didn't hesitate once because you want what's best for your little sister, even if it's not what's best for you. *That,* rather than your words from earlier, speaks volumes to your point. I'll consider this as I reflect on my own situation with Rory and others."

Liv nodded, realizing she shouldn't say another word. Bermuda had stated it perfectly. When we love someone, protecting what they want, even if it serves to take them away, is the greatest act of unconditional love.

CHAPTER FIFTEEN

Thankfully, Hester had agreed to meet Liv at her apartment to fix her finger. And even better was that she didn't ask any questions about how she'd gotten the injury. The healer was good like that.

Liv was grateful she didn't have to enter the House of Fourteen with the broken finger, possibly drawing unnecessary attention to her. Raina had been thoughtful enough to hide the inquiry from the Dragon Elite from the council, but that wouldn't last forever. Liv only had a few short weeks to cover up Sophia's egg. Then things would invariably unravel, with too many people asking questions and too many things she couldn't answer truthfully. Then everyone would know, and she'd have to face what came next.

But Liv breathed easily right now, knowing the fearful moment hadn't come yet. She flexed her fixed finger, feeling grateful as she entered the House.

The bright glow from the long corridor of statues made Liv squint. She wasn't sure if it was her imagination or lack of sleep, but the hallway seemed brighter somehow. Each time she entered the House, she found it different in little ways.

Her fingers ran over the language of the Founders that covered the golden walls. The message was still the same: Stop the One and you'll free us all.

Liv sighed. "Who is the One?"

"They say one is the loneliest number that you'll ever do," Plato said, popping up next to her.

"You're being particularly enigmatic lately," Liv observed.

"Why, because I'm quoting song lyrics?" he asked.

"That, and just about everything you're not telling me about."

"Yes, I'm glad you brought that up," Plato said, looking over his shoulder like he heard someone coming.

"Brought what up?" Liv asked, suddenly confused.

"Exactly," Plato said, continuing to stare over his shoulder. "So, I have to go somewhere for a bit."

"Somewhere?" Liv asked. "Like, you're taking a sabbatical? Did you book a nonrefundable vacation? Wait, is it another one of those deals you've made with a magical creature that you have to fulfill, like when you told my parents you'd watch out for me?"

"No, it's nothing like that. It's just that I need to go away for an unknown amount of time."

Not since hearing of her siblings' death had Liv felt such heartache. She was sure it materialized on her face, but she worked to cover it immediately. "This isn't really the best time for you to abandon me."

Liv was surprised by how hurt her voice sounded.

From the expression on Plato's face, he sensed it. For a brief moment, regret surfaced in his eyes.

"I know," he said simply, his tone gruff.

"We have the Mortal Seven to find."

"And *you* will find them," he said, swallowing hard.

"But you're always there," Liv argued. "When you say that you're going to be gone, you mean like invisible but still watching me, right? Like before?"

He shook his head. "I wish I could."

First Sophia, and now this. It was making it so Liv couldn't breathe properly.

"This is about the secret you're keeping, isn't it?" she asked.

Suddenly spooked, Plato jerked around, the hairs on his back standing on end. When he'd made certain there was nothing there, he turned back to Liv. "It is, but I still can't tell you."

"Because?" Liv challenged.

"Because there's no point and I'm running out of time. I really need to take my leave now," he said, a strange urgency in his voice.

"There *is* a reason to tell me. If you don't, I won't know why you've left. I'll worry. I'll think I've done something wrong. I'll—"

Plato shook his head. "There is nothing that you could ever do to make me leave you, Liv, and deep down, you know that."

There was that phrase again. "Deep down." Liv had said it to Bermuda, but hearing Plato say it now sparked something. It was something of supreme importance, but she couldn't figure out what or why.

Liv felt like a small child suddenly as she looked down at the lynx. He carried centuries of wisdom in his eyes, experience he had many times lent to her. What would she do without him? It seemed like she was losing a parent again.

"I'm not leaving you because I want to," Plato continued. "I haven't left your side in five years. But what I have to flee? Well, it's bigger than you or me."

"Tell me what it is," Liv urged. "We can fight this together."

He shook his head. "I wish we could. If there was another way, I'd tell you. But sometimes, things just can't be solved."

Tears ached in Liv's throat. She never allowed herself to cry, but right then, she wanted to let out all her fears and disappointments. She realized she'd been strong for so long; maybe this was what would finally break her.

Her eyes watered, but she caught the image of the lynx backing away, maintaining constant vigilance over his shoulder.

"When will I see you again?" Liv asked, realizing that the question should have been "Will I ever see you again?"

"I don't know," Plato said, and his voice was trembling with fear. Something was worrying him in a way she'd never seen before. "But please know that if I can find a way back to you, I will. And if I can't, I need you to know that serving the magical world alongside you has been the greatest honor of my very long life—"

"Plato…" Liv's voice shook too. The tears were coming, only a breath away now.

"Before you, I never much cared for helping others. It

was more of an obligation. And I was always a loner. A party of one. It's taken me this long to realize how wrong I was, and it's all because of you."

"How can you leave me, then?" Liv asked, a single tear running down her cheek.

The presence of the first tear seemed to pain Plato. He backed away, shaking his head. "I did not choose this, Liv. And I'll search with the time I have remaining to try to reverse this."

The floor trembled under Liv's feet, and she started. Plato jumped as well.

"I'm sorry, but I have to go now," Plato stammered. "Take care, Liv. I hope to see you again in this lifetime."

And as quickly as he had always materialized, the lynx disappeared, leaving Liv feeling raw and empty, and wondering if she'd ever see her best friend again.

CHAPTER SIXTEEN

The Black Void was completely different than Liv had ever seen it. White swirled in the blackness, and a strange smell seeped from the churning madness. It smelled of decay and mold. Liv covered her nose, turning away. It didn't interest her the same way it had before. Nothing did.

She turned her attention to the Door of Reflection, wishing there was some other way into the Chamber of the Tree. She would have rather crossed lava again to get in there rather than walk through a door that revealed her worst fears.

Liv knew all too well what her worst fears were because they were becoming her reality. Swallowing her reluctance, she stepped through the reflective surface.

In the dreamlike state, she stood in the middle of a barren desert with dark mountains in the far distance. Liv did a three-hundred-sixty-degree rotation. There was nothing out there. Just Liv and the desert and her loneliness.

She closed her eyes, knowing exactly what this fear was about. Being deserted by the ones she loved. Knowing there was no easy way to deal with this, Liv stepped all the way through the Door of Reflection into the Chamber of the Tree.

It warmed her heart slightly to see John staring at her from the bench, his kind eyes seeming to sense she was in pain. Stefan was busy giving a report about the Magic Playland, and all eyes were on him, except for John's.

Liv forced a smile, hoping to relieve his worry as she took her spot. Ireland Reynolds looked to be fitting right in between John and Raina, his cat Harry sitting on the table in front of him.

"This is incredible progress," Haro cheered. "Great work, Councilor Carraway."

"Thank you," John said, his focus still on Liv. "I'm afraid my leads have dried up for a bit, but I'm hoping that won't last long."

"Well, we count every victory," Raina stated. "Now, that brings us to the elf negotiations. Maybe one of the Mortal Seven will have an insight that will help us get past our normal roadblocks."

"What's wrong?" Stefan whispered to Liv as the council filled Ireland and John in on what had been transpiring with the elves. They still were reluctant to form a partnership with the House, and that was causing other races to rethink their support.

"I broke my finger," Liv lied.

His eyes darted to her mended hand. "I'm sorry. Is that why you look like you've been crying?"

Liv's eyes closed for a half-beat. She'd been so

distracted by everything that she'd forgotten to wipe the tears off her cheeks. She was certain her eyes were bright red, contrasting with her blue irises. "It was a pretty bad break."

"That's strange, because I've seen you get bitten by large serpents, fall great distances, and slashed by swords, and not even lose your appetite," Stefan said, a challenging look on his face.

Liv didn't feel like making her usual smart-ass reply. She felt her lips shake and pressed them together to cover it. "Sometimes it's the smallest things that break us," Liv said, thinking of little unsuspecting Plato, possibly gone forever.

Stefan offered her a sensitive smile. "I'm here if you want to talk about it."

"Thanks, I know you are," she said, grateful for him.

"And Warrior Beaufont," Hester stated. "Are you making progress with recovering the Mortal Seven?"

Liv coughed, realizing everyone's attention was suddenly on her. "Yes. I mean, not yet. I had other business to attend to, and since Kayla Sinclair is gone, I didn't think there was as much urgency to recover the next five."

"'Other business?'" Lorenzo questioned.

Raina looked down the bench at the other councilor. "We all know Liv works for Father Time."

"I didn't actually know that," Ireland stated, sounding impressed.

John elbowed him. "She's his assistant, in a way. Right-hand man...I mean, woman."

"To the father of time?" Ireland asked. "I didn't realize that was a real person. Does he live on a cloud?"

Liv wanted to laugh, but her current mood wouldn't allow it. "Not even close," she replied. "And as for the elf negotiations, I think I have an in that could help us. A way to mend bridges, if you will." She was working with Rudolf to set up a board meeting for his businesses with the elves. Hopefully, the time working together would soften them toward the House of Fourteen, but it was all a gamble.

"And what is that?" Bianca asked, her tone shrill and already disapproving.

"I really can't say," Liv stated, knowing full well that she could, but that keeping secrets would anger the Councilor.

"I must object to this type of—"

"Warrior Beaufont, I think your pocket is ringing," Haro said, pointing at her cloak.

Liv hadn't even realized it, too absorbed in her depression. "Oh!"

"Again, how many times do we have to tell you to put your phone on silent during these meetings?" Bianca stated, disapproval in her tone.

Liv pulled her phone from her pocket and was about to explain, but Hester cut her off.

"Warrior Beaufont is great about minding the rules, but she works for the one person who can break them all," the healer said, winking at her.

Hester was right. It was none other than Papa Creola calling. Liv held the phone to her head, not saying a word.

"Get to Subner's shop right now!" Papa Creola yelled into the phone, loud enough for everyone to hear.

Liv didn't answer vocally but did nod. "I have to go."

"Who is Subner?" Bianca asked.

"Your boyfriend," Liv stated matter-of-factly. Apparently, her humor hadn't taken as long a vacation as she'd expected. Diabolos, the black crow, materialized from the shadows, swooping down and landing at Liv's feet with a loud caw. She grimaced at the bird, who liked to call out her fibs.

"Really, Ms. Beaufont, you have strategies with the elves that you won't tell us about, get calls from Father Time during council meetings, and insult us without concern," Bianca stated, her head shaking.

"Liv only insulted you," Emilio, Bianca's brother countered.

Liv could have said a million hurtful things to Bianca Mantovani, but her own brother defending Liv seemed to be the worst thing ever. She narrowed her eyes, leaning forward. "Emilio, this doesn't involve you."

"You seem to say that a lot, sister," he fired.

Liv knew what this was about. Emilio was bitter that Bianca had disapproved of his relationship with a fae. It was one of the bigger problems Liv hoped to tackle when she had the time. Yes, she wanted to change the laws so Royals could date and marry other races. She wanted to be with Stefan in a real way. She wanted the House to be composed of more than just magicians and mortals, but all that would have to wait. She had to recover the Mortal Seven first. She had Sophia to think about. And now she had Plato to worry over.

"Actually, once I have a chance to meet with the elves," Liv began. "I'd like Emilio's help."

His eyes widened. Maybe he didn't realize that the meeting would be held in the fae kingdom, or maybe he was worried that his loyalty to her had gone too far.

"I'm happy to prove to the elves that I want their cooperation," Liv stated, reading the questions on the Councilors' faces. "However, King Dakota already trusts me. " She pulled out the navigation stone the king of the elves had given her when they'd met. "He also trusts Stefan since he worked to get rid of many of the elves' enemies. He doesn't trust pretty much anyone else in the House. We need to earn that, and the best way is to expose him to our Warriors and let him see that we all want to have their allegiance. We can't expect this to be easy, though. Decar murdered their people. Lorenzo insulted them—"

"I did what I thought—"

"You acted out of prejudice," John stated, cutting Lorenzo off. "And Liv is right; we need to undo those impressions the elves have of the House."

"But this will take time," Ireland stated.

Everyone but Bianca and Lorenzo nodded.

Liv's phone buzzed again in her hand. "I promise to work on finding the Mortal Seven and elf negotiations, but right now, I have to go."

Again, all except the two nodded as Liv hurried from the Chamber of the Tree.

CHAPTER SEVENTEEN

Roya Lane was more crowded than ever when Liv stepped through the portal. A large group was gathered around a figure she unfortunately recognized even from a far distance. It was hard to mistake the loud and flamboyant King Rudolf for anyone else.

Liv pushed through the crowd, mostly to make it to the other side where the Fantastical Armory was located at the end of the lane. However, as she passed Rudolf, she heard something that she couldn't entirely ignore.

"I'm getting something…" the fae said, his voice tentative at first. "Yes! Here it is. Your sister says she is well and misses you very much."

A woman with vibrant red hair pulled her hand from Rudolf's, shock covering her face. "But my sister isn't dead!"

Rudolf's smile dropped. "Oh, are you sure? How long has it been since you've spoken to her?"

"Well, not for a few weeks," the woman replied.

"You better try to reach her now, although I suspect it's too late," he stated gravely.

"Oh, dear. Oh, dear," the woman said, rushing from the crowd, shaking her head.

Liv pushed through the onlookers. "House of Fourteen business. Move aside." When she reached the front, Rudolf opened his arms wide. "Oh, my best friend, Warrior Beaufont. Did you want to talk to a passed relative?" His smile turned into a frown. "I'm not sure if I feel comfortable bringing back any of your relatives. Maybe you have an enemy you've slain in battle you'd like to apologize to?"

"I do not!" she stated adamantly, striding forward and grabbing Rudolf by the ear. "The show is over, people. Your king will be going with me."

Rudolf's feet moved double-time under him to keep up with Liv and not have his ear ripped off as she yanked him through the crowd. "I'm taking a five-minute break. Please form an orderly line, and I'll channel your dead when I return."

Liv didn't release the fae until they were far from the crowd, many of them watching them over their shoulders. "What is the meaning of this, King Dumbass?"

Rudolf rubbed his ear, a pained expression on his face. "I can talk to the dead."

For a half-beat, Liv's eyes closed. "No, Rudolf. No, you can't."

"Yes, I can!" he argued.

"Is this like that time you made a sandwich and Serena announced she was hungry a minute later, and you thought you could see the future?" she questioned.

"No. Well, sort of. You see, this morning, while doing

our fertility ritual where Serena steps over a dead man and then me—"

"Which is totally disgusting," Liv cut in.

Rudolf shot her a look of offense. "I don't see what's so strange about stepping over your own husband. It's probably being uptight like this that keeps you from getting married."

"Yes, that's the problem," Liv stated dryly.

"Anyway, I accidentally fell asleep during the ritual, which Bermuda stated could lead to a lazy child," Rudolf explained.

"Totally. That seems like a perfectly reasonable assumption."

"It's science, Liv," Rudolf protested.

"Yes, and I'm an astronaut."

"Oh, cool. Good to know. I might hit you up for a ride later. But for right now, will you stay focused? We're talking about me, not about you being a rocket doctor."

"There are so many things wrong with those sentences…but yes, please continue," Liv said.

"Anyway, I woke up suddenly, afraid I'd messed up the fertility practice. My hands flew out and I accidentally touched Serena, nearly tripping her. However, as soon as I had my wits about me—"

"Which took an act of God, right?"

Rudolf shot her a confused expression. "I don't know what you mean. But anyway, I got a very real message, not *from* Serena but rather *through* her. About her. It was from Gordon."

"Who was the dead guy lying beside you?" Liv asked, wondering why she was even having this conversation.

"Yes, exactly. We had to replace the last dead guy because he had started to smell," Rudolf explained.

"As they tend to do."

"Right," Rudolf said, nodding. "I knew the voice in my head was Gordon's. He was very clearly saying, 'I'm tired of doing this ritual.'"

"And after that moment, you assumed you could speak to the dead if you touched a living person they were trying to communicate with. Is that right?" Liv asked.

He nodded proudly. "So I decided to end the ritual and offer my talent to my people. Isn't that noble of me?"

Liv let out a deep breath. "Do you think it's entirely possible that you were the one tired of doing the ritual and you transferred that feeling onto Gordon?"

Rudolf shook his head. "No, I didn't even know Gordon. How would I know his likes and dislikes?"

"Ru, how long have you been lying on a floor and having Serena walk back and forth across you and a dead man?"

He began counting on his fingers. "Twice a day for three thousand steps. Carry the one. Divided by donut."

"Do you mean pi?" Liv asked.

He shook his head. "Wow, and you think *I'm* uneducated. You can't divide numbers by a pie. A donut is the number zero. That's obviously the right number for this equation."

"Right..."

"Anyway, we've been doing the ritual a lot. Let's just put it that way."

Liv nodded. "And although I know you want to have a child—"

"Need," Rudolf corrected. "Serena doesn't have that long. Maybe fifty years. Maybe sixty."

"Fine. You need to," Liv amended. "Do you think it's possible that you're tired of spending all your time doing these strange rituals?"

Rudolf scratched his head. "Well, when you put it that way, I guess Gordon and I have a lot in common."

Liv stopped her hand from strangling Rudolf. "No, I don't think you and Gordon have that much in common besides both being brain dead. I was insinuating that you don't want to spend all your time doing these fertility rituals."

The king of the fae seemed to consider this. "The floor is hard and has been hurting my back lately. And the dirt milkshakes I have to drink aren't that good. But if these things don't work, we're going to have to revert to something drastic."

"More drastic than including a dead man in your practices?" Liv asked.

He nodded. "Yes, and I'm not sure I'm up for marathoning DC Comics movies."

"Ummm, I'm unsurprisingly confused."

A loud sigh fell from his mouth. "Well, I'm a Marvel fan, and that's why—"

Liv held up her hand, halting him from saying another word. "I don't think there is anything you can say that will help me understand this any better. Why don't you quit doing all the fertility rituals? Just relax and focus on what you want. You know, a lot of people try and try, and actually conceive when they give up and adopt."

"But it's supposed to be tough for mortals and fae to mate," Rudolf reasoned.

"Yes, but you're a king. Just relax. It will happen."

He considered this and then nodded, a wide smile forming on his mouth. "Okay, Liv. That's what I'll do. I've tried literally almost everything else. Including wearing—"

Frantically, Liv shook her head. "I'm certain I don't need you to finish that sentence."

"Well, thanks for the help," Rudolf said, holding out his hand. "Would you like me to talk to anybody dead you know?"

Liv let out a steadying breath. "Of any of the people you touched, did you accurately read anything about their dead relatives?"

He thought for a moment. "Well, there was the woman who said she didn't have an Aunt Judy but did have an uncle who dressed in drag and I could have been mistaking her for him."

"That's what I thought," Liv stated. "I'm sorry to break it to you, but you can't speak to the dead. What you thought you heard Gordon say was actually *your* thoughts."

Rudolf clapped his hand to his mouth. "That makes so much sense." He let out a relieved breath. "This is good news. I was thinking I'd never be able to touch Serena again without hearing her Grandpa Joe tell me how hungry he was."

"Again," Liv said slowing, trying to quell her impatience, "when you touched Serena and heard this, were you by chance hungry?"

"Well, yes, but that's because we'd just got finished doing...well, you know..."

Liv nodded, swallowing to keep her lunch down. "Sure. I know what you mean."

Rudolf rubbed his stomach. "I don't know about you, but Pilates always makes me fiercely hungry."

"Wait, do you actually mean that you were doing Pilates?" Liv asked.

He gawked at her. "Yes. What did you think I meant?"

"Why didn't you just say you just got finished doing Pilates, instead of hinting at something more?"

"More?" Rudolf asked. "Like Pilates with TRX? What do you think I am? Insane?"

Liv's eyes fluttered with annoyance. "No, I'm obviously the one who is insane. And I have to get out of here. I'm already late."

"Okay, well, don't forget we have a board meeting coming up," Rudolf said, striding back to the crowd.

"I'll be there," Liv said, backing toward Subner's shop.

"And remember, it's your turn to bring the donuts," he reminded her.

"It's my first meeting," she stated.

"Yes, and that's how it works." He waved. "Besides, how are we going to do math if you don't bring the donuts?"

Liv thought about answering him but decided that there was absolutely no reason to. "Yeah, don't worry. I'll be there with donuts."

"Great!" he called. "I'll find a place for you to park your spaceship."

CHAPTER EIGHTEEN

Knowing she needed to make up for lost time, Liv sprinted all the way to Subner's shop. She didn't slow until she'd stumbled over the threshold, doubling over from having to weave around groups talking about the fae who spoke to the dead.

"H-h-hey," she stammered between breaths. "I'm here."

"I know," Subner said, not glancing up from his metalwork.

"I'm sorry I'm late. Kin—"

"Papa Creola knew you'd have to intervene with Rudolf," he stated matter-of-factly.

"So, what does that mean?" Liv asked, catching her breath as she strode into the shop.

"It means he knew exactly when you'd get here, and the timing was arranged based on knowing there would need to be an intervention in the Rudolf situation."

Liv rolled her eyes. "That's charming. So I was set up."

"Sure," Subner stated, eyeing the glowing red ball that

lay on the plate in front of him. It had just rolled out of a strange contraption onto a holder on the counter.

"All right, so I'm here. What does Papa need? I'm guessing he's gone, keeping it on the low down."

"I believe it's 'the down low,'" Subner corrected.

She shook her head. "I don't think so."

Ignoring her, Subner scooted off his stool and strode around the counter to the main showroom. "There's an ancient evil that's returned."

Liv yawned. "Man, this is how every day of my life begins."

Subner shot her a frustrated expression. "This is serious."

"Like when the SandMan came back and tried to put the mortals asleep?"

He shook his head. "No, not like that."

"Oh, then like when a Lophos attacked me, and I had to bring myself back from the dead?"

"Nope, not at all like that."

Liv sighed. "Oh, then is it like—"

"No, Warrior Beaufont," Subner cut her off. "It's like someone woke Cerberus, the three-headed dog who guards the underworld."

Liv paused. Gulped. Tried twice to compose herself. This was bigger than the SandMan. It was possibly bigger than anything she'd encountered thus far...maybe. "Oh, so is Cerberus going after mortals?"

Subner shook his head. "We call him Russ."

"That makes sense," Liv said, realizing Subner didn't find this as humorous as she did. "So is Russ going after mortals?"

"No," he answered. "He doesn't want mortals."

"Then Papa Creola, right?" she asked.

He shook his head again. "No."

"Okay, then I give up," she said, too overworked to play this game with the grumpy gnome. "Who is he after?"

"I can't tell you," Subner answered.

Liv nodded. "Again, that seems about right."

"All I can tell you is that it's a being as old as Russ. One who has lasted longer than they should have. Russ's job is to confine those who are supposed to be in the underworld there."

"Okay, so I'll go after him," Liv stated, ready to get started. She needed this mission to take her mind off Plato and wherever he was and wouldn't tell her.

"The thing is, you can't go after Russ yet," Subner stated.

"Of course, I can't," Liv replied dryly.

"First, I need you to go on an errand."

"Are you out of milk?" Liv asked.

He shot her a look of offense. "I'm lactose-intolerant."

"And I'm a jerk for not knowing that," she stated. "So what do you need?"

"I need the feather from the elusive phoenix," he said like he was simply asking her to stroll down to the market to pick up bread.

Liv let out an annoyed sigh. "Cool. And where do I find these elusive birds?"

"They are only known to reside on one island," Subner stated.

"Oh, well, that narrows it down, for once," Liv stated, slightly relieved.

"But they are tricky."

Liv sighed. "I'd expect no less."

"Recover one of their feathers and return to me promptly." He extended a hand.

She reached out, allowing him to drop something light into her palm.

"There you will find the unknown, uncharted location of the Phoenix. Please be careful, as there are many who will want to follow you, but only you must go. And once you're there, know that many will want to prevent you from your quest, knowing that the Phoenix is endangered and keeping it that way is important."

Liv unrolled the parchment and read. She nodded. "Yes, this seems about right."

CHAPTER NINETEEN

The island of Jaco was located where the Banda Sea and the Timor Sea meet, and it is therefore considered a sacred place by the natives. That was a good enough reason to keep people off the island, but it definitely wasn't the truth. What few knew was that this island in Indonesia was the only place the incredible Phoenix could be found.

The legendary birds, although harmless, was guarded by many dangerous creatures. Liv didn't know what those might be, since Bermuda Lauren's book, *Mysterious Creatures*, didn't go into detail. Apparently, the explorer had been too apprehensive to actually venture onto the island to research the bird. She was, of course, excited that Liv was going to go to the island, and asked her to take notes on the vegetation, local animal life, and of course, the Phoenix.

"*If*, and that's a big if, you return, I'll be happy to learn from your adventure," the giantess had said.

"Thanks for the well-wishes," Liv had replied before

hanging up the phone, realizing that Bermuda wasn't going to be any help at all.

Since portaling to the island wasn't an option, Liv had to hire a local native to boat her over to Jaco. Although it was considered sacred and visitors weren't allowed, for a wad of cash, the fisherman was happy to drop Liv off on the beach. When she asked about a ride back, the guy had waved her off, stating something about how that shouldn't be a problem.

"Like, you'll be back sometime soon?" Liv had asked him.

"Sure," he had said, appearing not completely honest.

"Just drive by on your way home this afternoon," Liv stated. "If you see me on the beach, please swing by and pick me up."

"Right," he answered, shaking his head.

Liv realized that most never left the island. She pictured a tomb of bones somewhere on Jaco, full of all the travelers who had never made it back to the beach to flag down the fishing boat to return home.

Once the fisherman sped away, leaving Liv alone on the island, she half-expected Plato to materialize as he usually did. For five years, he had been there even when she'd felt alone. Even at her lowest, she'd always had him. Even when she thought she couldn't escape a horrible evil or would die at the hands of a treacherous villain, Plato had always been there to save her. But that wasn't going to happen this time. For some strange reason, she could feel his total absence. It was like when the winds were stagnant. There wasn't anything missing that a person could point to, but for those looking for a bit of respite, they sorely missed that small, gentle breeze.

Liv's boot sank into the moist sand. She looked down at her all-black outfit, thinking she probably could have worn something a bit more practical to a deserted island with the scorching sun overhead.

"Like a casket," she joked morbidly as she peered at the trees in front of her. Several pairs of yellow eyes stared out of the darkness at her, blinking and shifting their gaze back and forth, almost as if they were communicating with one another.

Liv was going to pull Bellator when she ventured under the dark canopy of the trees. However, she decided it was probably best not to be on the offensive upon entering the jungle. Liv imagined that many tough guys had probably raided the island, showing their weapons and muscles, looking tough. Whatever protected Jaco and the phoenix wouldn't be impressed by her giant-made sword. If anything, that would make whatever it was more likely to attack.

Instead, Liv should show the island's residents that she wasn't a threat. She began whistling like she was casually strolling through a garden. She was only there to get a single feather from a phoenix. She had learned from *Mysterious Creatures* that the phoenix was worshipped in Egypt, but ironically not at all close to that area.

Legend had stated that only one phoenix could exist at a time. Upon its death, it would burst into flames, and a new phoenix would take its place. Or the same one. There wasn't a lot known about the elusive bird. All Liv knew for sure was that they were a symbol of immortality, which was strange, since after this she had to go after Russ, who was hunting a being who had cheated death for a long time, apparently.

The jungle was so dark that Liv had to stop for her eyes to adjust. She was strangely seeing spots from being in the bright sun on the ocean. After closing her eyes for half a beat, she found it much easier to see.

She went to take a step forward, but her foot was stuck. Looking down, Liv didn't see her boots. They had sunk into the soft sand. Quicksand.

CHAPTER TWENTY

L iv had watched enough eighties movies to know that
struggling would only make her sink faster. She
wasn't sure why, but everyone seemed to get trapped in
quicksand in older movies. Maybe that was before they'd
concreted everything, getting rid of much of the deadly
danger.

That's what this island needs, Liv thought bitterly. *Side-
walks. And maybe a Starbucks.*

The sand, which was much more like mud than
anything else, was quickly rising. It was already up to her
knees. Liv pulled out Bellator, not only because it was
weighing her down, but because it was probably her only
hope of getting out of the sandpit alive. As far as she could
tell, she was solidly in the middle of it, with fifteen feet
dividing her from any place of safety. The closest tree or
branch was farther because that made for a perfect trap.

She held Bellator over her head like a spear and
launched it. The sword stuck several yards away, landing

with a satisfying thud, shaking back and forth. To her relief, it didn't sink.

"Now I just need some rope," Liv muttered, wondering if she could conjure some. When her hands remained empty after trying three times, she realized that she couldn't. There was a protective spell around the quicksand, it seemed. Whatever was protecting the phoenix and the island had thought this far ahead, at least.

"Okay, how about a vine?" Liv mused, pointing at the canopy overhead. Not just a rope of vine fell down on her head, but along with it came a few heavy branches, which assaulted Liv in the head, making her sink faster.

She threw them off the best she could, but then saw the hole she'd made in the canopy overhead. It hurt her heart, making her realize she'd damaged the forest. Even though she knew conserving her magic was best, she made an impromptu decision. Pointing at the branches, she sent all of them, minus one long vine, back up, weaving them back into place.

When that was done, she turned her attention to the vine, trying to wind it up, careful to keep it from the quicksand. Liv wasn't sure how her lasso skills were since she hated rodeos and had spent exactly zero time as a cowgirl.

Holding onto one end, she tried to toss the vine at Bellator. Thankfully, her aim was good, and the vine made contact. Unfortunately, her approach was wrong, and the vine simply fell loose beside Bellator.

Liv huffed, looking down. The quicksand was at her hips now.

"Okay, I just need to focus," she decided, letting out a long breath.

Like she'd seen in the movies, Liv circled the vine over her head, releasing it when it had enough speed. It actually wrapped around Bellator, to her surprise. However, when Liv tugged, it pulled free again.

She reeled it in quickly, not at all entertained by the gross noises the quicksand was making. Again Liv tried to lasso Bellator, but the pressure caused by sinking seemed to be deterring her from focusing properly.

Beside her, the trees shook. She was doubtful it was a park ranger who was coming to help. When a giant lizard crashed through the brush, Liv lost hope that he was there to save her.

The thing was easily as long as a car. Its long forked tongue slipped from its mouth as it regarded her with ravenous fury.

"Die by quicksand or giant lizard?" Liv asked herself, tilting her head back and forth as if weighing her options.

Wondering why she hadn't considered this before, she pointed her finger at the vine's end lying next to Bellator. It rose, circling several times before tying itself in place. Liv tugged, finding the vine secure.

She began pulling herself toward Bellator as the lizard lumbered in her direction, looking not at all happy about her attempts to escape. As she neared the edge of the quicksand, the beast sped up, moving with more agitation.

Liv redoubled her efforts, moving her hands one over the other as she dragged her legs behind her. The lizard, who had no manners whatsoever, tried to cut her off when she made it to the dry bank, lashing out at her.

Liv was forced to drop the vine as she launched a fireball at the monster. He swallowed it promptly, gulping it down like it was a large turkey.

"Right," Liv said. "So you like fire. Good to know."

The lizard opened his mouth, and a rush of flames sped out of it. Liv jumped, ducking and wrapping her arms over her head as the heat soared over her. The momentum had been enough to release her from the quicksand, but now she had bigger problems. Literally.

The giant lizard closed his mouth, blinking at her with a strange fury. Liv didn't want to do what seemed like the obvious thing, but she knew she had little choice. Fire didn't work on the beast. He was too close to Bellator for her to reach. And her only other option rested next to her.

Liv stuck out her hand, throwing a huge wave of wind at the lizard. As she'd planned, it picked him up as if it were a cyclone, whirled him around, and dropped the flailing monster into the pit of sand where she'd just been.

The lizard screamed, its claws paddling frantically as its bottom half sank. The sight was too much for Liv. She wanted to live and didn't want to be eaten by the man-eating lizard, but killing it, especially like this, seemed wrong.

She strode quickly over to Bellator, pulling it up from the earth.

"I might regret this," she said, pointing at the lizard that was about to be swallowed by the quicksand because it hadn't watched enough movies and didn't know to remain still.

Liv pressed her eyes shut and pulled her hand back up as if yanking in a fish at the end of a line. The lizard flew toward her and knocked her back, and she crashed into a tree trunk. And because she had that kind of luck, the lizard landed only a few feet away, adorned with quicksand all over his body, the same as Liv.

She rubbed her head from the impact, giving the lizard a tentative expression. "So, I'm not sure if you realized what happened there, but in case you blacked out, I just saved your life."

The lizard lunged at her. She jumped back, narrowly avoiding being chomped.

"Sure, I was the one who threw you in the quicksand, but still, I saved you," Liv argued.

Again the beast lunged at her. Liv decided against an attack. For some reason, Bellator wasn't interested in fighting the beast, which was unlike the blood-hungry sword. Instead, it seemed to want to rest. Knowing that trusting her sword was for the best, Liv stuck it in her sheath, staring at the lizard like it had the next move.

"I'm unarmed," she stated. "So if you're going to eat me, do it fast. I don't have time for you to find hot sauce, which obviously makes everything taste better."

Liv stared at the lizard, waiting for its next move. She was prepared to jump to the side. To run. To fly into the trees. But what she knew she must *not* do was hurt the lizard. That message was echoing from her core. The lizard didn't lunge. Instead, it approached her, sniffing her boots. She tensed, clenching every muscle in her body. She kept her chin up as the lizard ran its nose up to her hips, continuing to sniff.

"Good lizard," Liv said, wondering if it was deciding where to start eating her. Maybe one arm at a time? Maybe from the head down? Or the feet up?

It flicked its long tail, creating a wind that was almost as strong as the one she'd used to knock it into the sandpit. Again, the tail flew. It was about to hit her in the face. Liv didn't back away, though. A strange faith overcame her, and she remained completely still as the tail soared straight for her face.

To her surprise, it stopped inches away. She held her breath. Blinked. Nearly peed herself. Then slowly, the lizard lowered his tail, regarding her with quiet appreciation. His tongue flicked out of his mouth as he sauntered into the jungle, apparently done with her.

"Well, that was easy," Liv lied, brushing at the quicksand on her pants, to zero effect. She looked around, hearing a rustling sound, wondering what devilish monster was after her next.

Liv didn't pull Bellator when the trees parted as if being pushed apart by giant hands. Instead, she lowered her chin and waited for whatever was going to come next.

For the second time, Liv almost wet herself when a glorious and majestic orange and red bird as large as an eagle soared over the trees and landed on the ground before her. The bird had bright blue eyes and all the wisdom of the world in his gaze. Liv had never seen anything so beautiful in all her life.

And then he spoke to her, not aloud, but rather in her mind.

You know when to not fight and how to honor and protect all creatures, the phoenix said. *I have yet to meet anyone who visits my island like you.*

The phoenix flew away without another word, but

lying where it had been was a single orange and red feather. Liv could hardly believe it.

She approached carefully, worried this a trick. However, when she held the feather in her hands, it was real.

Had everyone who had ever come to Jaco Island fought and pillaged, looking for the feather? Was the key to be at peace with the island, not fighting the dangers it presented? Liv wasn't sure she'd ever know what had transpired on that strange island, but as she held the feather close to her chest, she was aware that she'd been in the presence of one of the most powerful creatures in the magical world.

CHAPTER TWENTY-ONE

L iv deposited the phoenix's feather on the countertop in front of Subner. If he was impressed, he didn't show it.

"So you didn't fight the monitor lizard, then?" Subner asked.

Liv narrowed her eyes at him. "I did, sort of. But then I rescued him."

"And you didn't destroy the forest to get out of the quicksand?" Subner asked curiously.

"I did, but I mended it," she replied bitterly.

He nodded, combing his hand over his chin. "Did you meet any of the other creatures guarding the island?"

"No, and if you knew about all this, why didn't you warn me?" Liv asked.

"Because," Subner began, "the phoenix would have known if you were doing something to be proven as being noble at heart. You can fake that, but it's detectable. I needed you to be honest and good because that was what you wanted to be. Because you knew preserving life was important. That was the only way the phoenix would relinquish one of its feathers."

"If I had defended myself, like, killed the lizard and brought down a tree, what would have happened?" Liv asked.

"More obstacles would have come at you until you were dead."

"And you just let me walk into that without any warning?" Liv questioned, her voice rising.

"I had confidence that you'd make the right decisions," Subner stated, plucking the feather off the counter and turning back to his work with the two metal balls.

"You and Papa are some tricky—"

"I'd stop while you're ahead, Warrior Beaufont," Subner stated.

"Okay, fine. I'm still alive. Thanks for not telling me how to survive because that might have gotten me killed…I think."

"And now you're ready to go stop Russ," Subner said. "Although it will be much more difficult than getting the feather from the phoenix."

"Let me guess: you're not going to tell me how to defeat him, even though you know, right?"

"I actually don't know," Subner said with a sigh. "It's been a long time since Russ was around."

"Oh, well, I realize you told me he's after a powerful entity," Liv began. "But my question is, why?"

"Because Papa Creola cares a great deal about this creature," Subner stated.

Liv was surprised he had given her any information. "Continue," she dared to say.

"I believe that whoever released Russ wants to draw Papa Creola out of hiding, thinking he will defend this creature from Russ," Subner explained.

"But he won't, will he?" Liv questioned.

Subner shook his head. "No, he's relying on you to do it."

Liv nodded. "Okay, so where do I find Russ?"

"The portal to the underworld is in a place few expect," Subner stated. "However, Russ won't be there for long unless you stop him. Once he breaks out, he'll come after his target and carry it to where he believes it belongs—the underworld, where it will be trapped forever."

"Okay, so is the portal to the underworld at Disneyland? Or a frozen yogurt shop? Another happy place?" Liv asked.

"No, it's in a place much happier than those." Again, he extended his hand. She copied his movement, allowing him to drop another piece of parchment into her palm.

Liv unrolled it, read the location, and realized she should be surprised. However, at this point, this was par for the course.

CHAPTER TWENTY-TWO

Canada. Obviously, the portal to the underworld was located in the peaceful and happy country of Canada. Specifically, it was in a little village where the locals all knew each other's names and played ice hockey together on the weekends. The portal was apparently in the cellar of a craft mall, where the locals all rented booths to display their art and sold it to one another.

According to the owner, Amity Buckwell, no one ever made any money because they always turned around and bought something from another artist with their profits.

"We mostly just trade funds," Amity explained.

"That's sweet," Liv said, admiring the various booths as she passed them on the way to the back.

Amity hadn't questioned Liv when she stated that she needed to inspect the cellar. She'd simply smiled and said she'd be happy to show Liv anything she needed to see. Liv wanted to caution the woman to ask for ID in the future or something, but that kind of questioning would have prevented Liv from getting to the portal.

Maybe Amity didn't know her shop's cellar led to the underworld. Maybe she did know, and thought that whoever was bold enough to venture down there had to endure the risk that went along with it. Or maybe all Canadians were just good people.

"I'll take it from here," Liv said when Amity unlocked the door to the musty cellar.

"Whatever you like," the woman said, holding up the keys. "I'll be up in my office if you need anything. Just holler when you're done, and I'll come down here and lock up."

Liv nodded, forcing a smile. She turned for the door but paused. "Do you know what's down here?" Her curiosity had finally gotten the better of her.

The woman's expression changed. "I've heard rumors, but I treat this area of the building the same way I do bell peppers."

"How is that?" Liv asked.

"I leave them alone. The darn things give me heartburn, and are too spicy for my liking."

Liv nodded. Canadians couldn't even handle a bell pepper. The extra jalapenos she ordered on her nachos would probably kill them. "So you know what's down there, then?"

"I know what my granny told me," Amity answered. "She's the one I inherited the business from. I've done what she told me and kept the area locked at all times. However, she said that if anyone ever showed up needing to go down there, I was to let them in without question."

That had made Liv's job easier. "Well, I'm here to secure

it so it doesn't get out, which is what I suspect it will do if it goes unchecked."

Amity shivered. "I appreciate that very much. I'd never get to sleep at my usual bedtime of seven-thirty if I knew ghosts were roaming the streets."

Ghosts. That was what Amity thought was locked in the cellar? And seven-thirty? These people were simple but in wonderful ways.

"Don't worry," Liv stated confidently. "I'll ensure the ghosts stay locked down here."

Amity smiled in relief. "I'm glad for that. I just wonder who called you to tell you about the problem. Murray, maybe? He's the one who has been hearing the ghosts get more restless, probably because his booth is closest."

Liv nodded. "Yes, it was Murray."

Amity backed away. "Well, you do your job, and I'll go do mine."

Once the woman was gone, she turned to face the eerie darkness that lay before her. The stairs to the cellar descended rapidly, leading to what she could tell was a dank and dirty storage area. Liv knew exactly what she was going to face, but the question that plagued her the most was why?

Why was Russ back? Who was he after? And why was this creature so important to Papa Creola?

Pulling Bellator from its sheath, she started down the rickety steps, knowing the best way to find answers was to search for them. Nothing was ever revealed in a beacon of light, but rather after exploring the darkness where few ventured.

The step shuddered under Liv's boots. She was about to conjure a light when a flame on the stone wall ignited. Liv's hands automatically tightened on Bellator, and she paused to study the strange blue flame. This place was full of magic, and a very strange kind, too.

Tentatively, Liv took a step, and another flame materialized on a torch ahead. She could now see that the staircase led to a wet stone floor surrounded by brick walls pierced by barred doors. At the end was the largest door, and behind it, something stirred. This definitely wasn't the most inviting place she'd ever been.

Water dripped from the rafters overhead. The floor shook again when Liv made it to the bottom of the stairs. She didn't jump when something knocked hard against the barred door ahead. However, she nearly sliced Plato in half with Bellator when he materialized beside her.

"What the hell?" she asked, her anger flaring. He had never startled her when he popped up randomly, but that was because she was usually half-expecting it. However, he had left her, and she hadn't thought he'd be coming back anytime soon. As happy as she was to see him, she was also furious that he had scared her so badly.

"You can't go down there," he said, his voice deadly serious.

"What?" she questioned. "I have to. Papa Creola says I have to stop Russ from getting out, which it sounds like he almost is."

Plato nodded. "He's broken through the first four gates. There's only one left."

Liv let out a long breath. "Well then, it sounds like I better hurry."

"No, you can't." Plato moved faster than she'd ever seen him, taking the place in front of her and blocking her path.

Liv narrowed her eyes at the lynx. "You've been acting super-strange lately. You leave me without an explanation, and now you've shown up and told me I can't do my job."

"Liv, I think you can do many amazing things. However, you can't stop Russ. He's too powerful, and he will kill anyone who gets in his way."

Heat flared across her face. "How dare you tell me I can't do this? I've fought things that make this puppy look like...well, like a puppy dog."

"With three heads," Plato said, walking backward, looking over his shoulder at the thundering gate.

Liv followed. "Why did you show up now? I thought you said you had to disappear? Did you just stop by to tell me I'd fail, and that I can't do this?"

"Liv, this is the strongest magical creature I've ever known. There is only one creature who has ever defeated it."

"The one who put it behind the five gates, right?" Liv guessed.

Plato nodded.

"Well, who was it? Maybe I can go and find them," she said, mostly to herself. If Plato hadn't deserted her, he could have given her this information originally and saved her the time.

"They can't help you," he explained. "They aren't as powerful as they used to be, and the fight to send Russ back to the underworld, behind the gates, would kill them."

Liv lowered her chin, frustration building in her head. "Plato, tell me what's going on now. I'm tired of the secrets and the mystery."

He sat on his haunches and looked up at her. "Russ wants me."

Her mouth fell open. Shock made her knees soften. "What?"

"I'm the one who locked him behind the five gates," Plato stated. "He came after me when I didn't die the first time. It's against the rules. When someone dies, they are sentenced to the underworld. Russ keeps them there. However, my existence breaks that rule. Unlike Papa Creola, I'm not a god of any sort. I simply defy the laws."

"Because you have nine lives or something?" Liv asked, lowering Bellator.

"More like a hundred," he stated. "When Russ came after me the first time, I fought him, using up a few of my lives. However, I was able to push him behind the five gates and put him to sleep. Someone woke him, though, and he's madder than hell. He's coming after me."

"Which was why you left me," Liv guessed.

"I didn't want to," he said on the heels of her statement.

"But if you fought him before, then why can't you now?"

"It's the same reason I've been acting differently," Plato stated.

Liv thought about how he was showing up more when he normally disappeared around most people. He'd also been saying things that bordered on sentimental. And then there was the secret he didn't want to tell her. The tears suddenly welled up in her throat. She held her breath, knowing with absolute certainty what he hadn't wanted to tell her.

"You're down to your last life, aren't you?"

With a piercing pain in his eyes, he nodded. "I'm sorry, Liv."

"Y-y-you're sorry?" Liv stammered. "Why are you apologizing to me? You're the one who is..."

She couldn't say it. Dying. They both knew the word, but neither spoke it.

"I hadn't realized you'd put yourself in so much danger lately," Liv said.

"My lives work a bit differently," he explained. "Yes, I lose them if I'm mortally injured. However, the magic that created me is unique, and so powerful that it is shrouded in mystery in order to protect it from being stolen. That's the law that governs my life. So when you've seen me shift or do anything outside my normal parameters, it has taken one of my lives."

Liv's mouth fell open. Her tongue was suddenly dry. "So when you saved me from the mermaid and I briefly spied you as a lion..."

He nodded. "And when I rescued you in griffin form from the Matterhorn. Anytime someone saw my magic, it cost a life."

Liv had known for some time that if Plato revealed his secrets, it weakened him, but she never would have guessed this. "So you literally killed yourself every time you saved me."

"I would do it all over again, exactly the same way," he said firmly.

"But you only have one life left," she said, hardly able to speak past the tears.

"Which wouldn't be a problem," he stated, "but Russ is awake now, and he's coming for me. One attack from him, and I'm gone."

"Then I definitely have to stop him," Liv said, real conviction in her tone.

"No!" Plato yelled. The gate shook again. In the distance, Liv suddenly spied several small lights. Then she realized that they weren't lights, but rather eyes. Three pairs of eyes.

Plato didn't turn to look at the monster banging on the gate behind him. "You won't be able to defeat him. I can't have you risking your life for this."

"You risked yours for me. You lost lives for me."

"And I've lived for centuries," he argued. "I've had lots of time on this planet. You are young, and the world needs you."

"I need you," she countered. "And when I stop Russ, you'll have, what? Fifteen or twenty years, right?"

"Roughly," he answered.

Deep growls echoed from the end of the hallway. It was hard to make out Russ on the other side of the bars, but Liv could definitely see the whites of his teeth

Liv stepped to the side, narrowing her eyes at the rusty barred door. "I'm doing this, Plato. If Russ is here, you shouldn't have even shown up."

"No matter what I do, he'll find me," he stated. "I had hoped to hide for a little while, but I knew it was a long shot."

"And that's why I'm going to put him back in his cage."

"Liv, please!"

She shook her head and charged forward. "Don't try to stop me. I want you out of here now. Get as far from Russ as possible."

"Liv," he pleaded.

She spun, determination written on her face. "I've never demanded anything of you, Plato, but right now, I'm ordering you to get out of here. Don't try to stop me. I've made up my mind."

"But pushing him back and putting him to sleep is incredibly difficult," he argued.

A mischievous smile whisked to her face. "I know. Which is why I'm going to kill him."

CHAPTER TWENTY-THREE

The sound of her boots on the wet floor echoed loudly. She was able to make out a large black form pacing in front of the gate as she got closer. The movements were rough and full of hostility, but the mutt had stopped ramming the gate. Liv figured she'd simply stab him in the heart through the bars and be done with it.

She looked over her shoulder. Plato was gone. He had listened to her.

It was hard for her to believe he'd lost so many lives for her, but everything made sense now. His mystery, him hiding his magic and his secrets.

Papa Creola had assigned her this case, which meant that he didn't want anything to happen to Plato either.

Liv knew that killing the beast wasn't the most desirable option. He did have a role in the world, keeping the dead in the underworld. It was honorable that Plato had simply caged him and put him to sleep, but it obviously wasn't a long-term option. She'd made up her mind. No matter the consequences, she was going to kill the guardian of the underworld.

A chorus of low growls greeted her when she neared the barred gate.

"Hey, boys," she called when she could make out the shapes of the black dog's faces. The heads were wolf-like, with their pointy ears and long snouts. The beast was massive, the width of the big gate, and he towered over her.

Even though it was dark, Liv could plainly see the creature's chest. "I realize that you three have a job to do, and you're just doing it. The thing is, I have a job to do also, and it involves protecting my friends, no matter what the cost."

The three heads growled louder, their eyes glowing red. Liv pulled back Bellator, ready to strike the dog through the bars. The beasts opened their mouths, and rather than growling again, fire shot out, sending her stumbling back to avoid getting caught in the flame. She fell on her backside and shuffled back on her hands and feet, pulling Bellator with her.

The fire dissipated from their mouths but re-surfaced in their eyes. Behind their heads, fire licked at the air, emitting black smoke all around them.

Striking Russ in the chest was going to be harder than Liv thought if the monster could spit fire at her—an important tidbit she thought Plato could have mentioned, if only in passing.

Liv pushed up, dusting herself off as the heads jerked from side to side, almost as if fighting each other.

"Good. A little internal rivalry might be the distraction I need," Liv said, twirling Bellator around and locking it in place with both hands as she sidestepped forward again.

A snarl ripped from the head on the far left, and it lunged at the one in the middle. The head on the right opened his mouth. Liv prepared to be blasted by fire again, but this time the flames flowed out of its mouth and behind it. Russ was on fire from the inside out. Its emotions seemed to communicate this internal raging fire that spread over the dog more with each passing second.

The other two heads continued to fight, biting at each other and jerking their shared body from side to side. Liv would have taken this opportunity to strike, but the head on the right was keenly focused on her.

The two fighting heads gave Liv an idea. She raised her hand, about to spell them, when the head on the right lowered, steam rising from his nostrils. The beast raised his paw, covered in long, sharp claws, and slammed it into the gate. Liv barely had time to react, throwing herself against the brick wall to the side and shielding her head. The barred door flew straight back through the hallway, slamming into the stairs and breaking them into pieces.

The two fighting heads forgot their dispute as the beast realized it was free. It stepped over the threshold that had been barred by the last gate. Cerberus, the guardian of the underworld, was at large...and madder than hell.

CHAPTER TWENTY-FOUR

L iv glanced back at her only exit. The stairs had been demolished. She knew that portaling out of there wasn't an option. The area was blocked from teleporting, which was why Amity had to let her in.

That was fine, Liv thought. *I don't plan on running, not when I have a job to do.*

She stepped out from beside the brick wall into the center of the long hallway and faced the slowly approaching beast.

Russ appeared to be slightly disoriented by his first taste of freedom in centuries. He took each step carefully, his long claws raking the bricks.

Now that the dog was free, Liv could plainly see how large he was. The animal was about the size of a horse, with a long tail that swished back and forth, accurately communicating its hostility.

Liv ran through her options. She was a bit peeved at herself for thinking she could simply stab the magical creature in the chest and be done with it, but simple solutions were usually the best. That was why she thought her second idea still might be worthwhile. However, she needed a distraction since all three heads were lowered and all six eyes were focused on her.

Methodically, Russ raised one paw, sliding it forward as he took another step. He knew she had nowhere to go. She knew he was stalking his prey, figuring out how best to attack. They both knew one of them wasn't getting out of this alive.

Liv took one hand off Bellator. Four of the six eyes narrowed as she held her palm out, watching each of her movements keenly. A fireball materialized in her hand, starting out small, the size of a golf ball. It quickly gained size and speed, growing bigger than a softball and rotating so quickly that it was mostly a blur.

"Hey, Rover! Do you want to play fetch?" Liv asked, earning a contemptuous growl from two of the heads. The one on the right wasn't distracted like the others. It seemed to be the mastermind.

Liv laughed, thinking how perfect the expression was for that particular head.

When Russ looked to be on the verge of charging, Liv released the fireball, aiming it to the left of the beast. It sped past, gaining the attention of two of the heads. The other, more focused one, lost the battle and was jerked in the opposite direction and dragged back to where they'd busted through the gate.

It skidded to a halt as the fireball exploded in the darkness, sending sparks and debris in all directions.

The head on the right looked over its shoulder, its fiery eyes full of hatred.

Yeah, I've pissed off that one, all right, Liv thought, funneling all of her energy and focus into a very specific spell. When she was sure it was right, she directed that energy at the two heads on the left.

The curse left her fingers like a comet, streaking down the hall and circling the two heads, clouding them in dust for a moment. When it dissipated, Liv held her breath, not knowing for sure if the spell had worked. There was only one way to tell.

The head on the right, tugged the others so they were all three facing Liv. It growled low, and the others copied the sound. Fire flared in their eyes and poured from their mouths.

Liv had gambled, and she had been certain it was a good idea. However, the spell didn't seem to have worked, and it had taken a huge chunk of her reserves. She was going to have to rely on her strength to battle Russ, but based on his size and the number of teeth he had bared at her, she doubted she'd get a hit in before he slaughtered her.

The monster lifted his paw, holding it up. All he had to do was lunge and strike to end her world. She lifted her own hand, copying his movement. Her magic was weak, and her head was beating with the heat. She could think of only a couple of spells that might help her, but all of them required more than she had left.

Still, she wasn't going to quit now. Then she'd be dead, and soon after, so would Plato. That wasn't an option.

She tried to figure out what her options were. Fire wouldn't work, and many other attacks were too much for her at that point. But the element that magicians controlled was available to them for much less effort. It might not work, but what did she have to lose at that point?

With her hand still raised, she released a gust of wind, throwing it straight at Russ. It rushed at the creature, and when it was just about to strike him, the beast swiped his paw, simply and effectively knocking it down with little effort.

And that was it. Liv had tried everything she could think of. She was down to almost nothing. She lifted Bellator, feeling its familiar hungry pulse in her hands. She might be down to her last option, but she wasn't out yet. She and Bellator would fight to the end.

Liv gritted her teeth, about to lunge forward and attack Russ with everything that she had left. She had rocked back on her heels in preparation when the head on the left yelped so loudly the building shook. The head in the middle lunged at its brethren again, biting his ear completely off.

Liv backed up, her eyes wide at the disgusting sight in front of her.

It had worked! She couldn't believe it. The feuding spell she thought had failed had only been delayed, and it appeared the two heads were ready to fight until the bloody end, which might be sooner rather than later.

The head on the left sent blood all over the stone walls. It splattered Liv's face as it shook. Its ear was missing, but that wasn't stopping it from fighting back. It teeth clacked loudly as it tried to attack the one in the middle. The head on the right seemed to know who was responsible.

It shot Liv a murderous look, fire flaring in its eyes. Thankfully, the fight of the other two knocked the dog off balance, sending it into a roll. Claws and fangs flashed through air filled with smoke and fire.

Liv watched, backing up as the fight got closer to her. When her heel met the rubble that used to be the stairs, she realized she was officially out of options. The beast was too large to get by without getting swept up in the fight. Her magic reserves were too low for her to hover or fly to the door, which was one story up.

The head on the left let out a ferocious growl that rocked the building, sending loose bricks from overhead raining down. Liv covered her head, diving as the rest of the stairs collapsed. She rolled, finding herself inches from Russ's feet.

Her breath stopped. Her pulse quickened. Cold sweat ran down her forehead. "Nice doggy," Liv said, holding Bellator in front of her. She realized that one strike from Russ would end her.

The head on the right opened his mouth, infernal fire roaring deep inside of him. Liv lifted Bellator, knowing that was her last option. Then the head in the middle thrust itself to the left, taking the weight of the beast with it, slamming the other head into the stone wall.

A loud and guttural scream filled the air, followed by cracking. Bricks rained down again. The cellar was a mess of dust and smoke. Liv blinked, trying to figure out what had happened. It took her several moments to make out the strange shape of the dog. It appeared quite different when it lunged to the side, away from the broken wall.

The head on the left was limp, the fire in its eyes gone, blood pouring from the hole in its head. It was dead.

The head in the middle was battered from slamming its

brethren into the wall. It was also disoriented. The head on the right seemed to be trying to pull the body upright, but the balance was completely off.

This was Liv's chance.

She straightened, holding Bellator close to her chest, then she shot forward, whipping her sword up and diagonally. As she'd planned, the disoriented head was too slow to react. It merely blinked, not moving fast enough before her blade ripped through the soft underside of its neck. She sliced through cleanly, killing the middle head at once. Like the one beside it, it was bloody and limp, its fire extinguished.

Liv's chest rose and fell as the beast lumbered to the side like a drunken sailor trying to find their way. The one remaining head was having trouble balancing, which would make finishing it easy.

Liv smiled, holding Bellator proudly. She raised the sword, thinking that finishing this beast was the kind thing to do.

"Thank you for your service, but it's time that you rested forever," Liv said. She brought Bellator down, but before it connected with the last head, a blast of hot wind shot from the dog's mouth. It threw her back, making her slam into the broken staircase. She lost Bellator in the blast, and her head hit something hard. Fire erupted all around her, or at least, that was what it felt like. She saw ash and smoke, and her eyes burned. She had no idea what was happening. When her vision cleared, she realized how wrong she'd been to think this was over.

The two heads turned to ash from the top down. The remaining head shook, causing the ash to fall to the floor.

There, standing completely untouched and unfettered by the dead heads, was Russ, eyes full of fire, a solid and incredibly huge dog who looked ready to fight for centuries.

And she was bruised, weaponless and without a single option left.

CHAPTER TWENTY-FIVE

"And this is exactly why two heads aren't better than one," Liv found herself saying as she tried to stand.

Something was wrong with her back. And her front. And her head. She was pretty sure she'd broken a rib. Not to mention that every part of her mentality felt broken too as she stared into the soulless eyes of the beast before her.

The other heads that had been weighing Russ down had vanished. Now he was a giant wolf, with every advantage and renewed strength.

When Liv drew a breath, she choked on her own blood. *That wasn't good.*

The beast growled. It sounded like an ancient language full of curses and promises, ones that would confine her to her own personal hell for all of eternity.

She ran through her options. She had no sword, no magic, and hardly any strength. At this point, all she had was her negotiation skills, and she doubted those would do much against a hellhound.

"I-I-I," Liv stuttered, choking up more blood. She was

pretty sure her lungs had been punctured. She didn't have long to live at this rate, so maybe it was better that the beast take her out.

When he lifted his head to the ceiling and let out a victorious howl, Liv's chest vibrated with a fear unlike any she'd ever known. And then something orange and massive sprang. Her instinct told her to look away, but she didn't. Not in time.

She watched as Plato in the form of a lion soared through the air. He was large. Majestic. Hulking. He was everything a great hero should be, the stuff of legends. As his teeth sunk deep into Russ's throat, Liv felt she watched every victory of every great hero ever.

The beast screamed and then rolled, but Plato didn't let go. He sank his teeth in deeper and ripped up and out, opening the dog's throat and ending it with one solid movement. There was no mercy, and there was no terror. This was the act of a true champion. One who knew how to end things the right way.

However, relief didn't flood Liv's body when Plato looked up, blood covering his large mouth as he stood atop his kill. Instead, she read the look in his eyes and knew what this victory had cost him.

Her lips shook. Her chest vibrated. Tears filled her eyes.

She staggered forward. Fell at the lynx's feet just as it shrank back down to its normal size.

Before her, he was tiny once more. It was wrong and beautiful at the same time

"You sh-sh-shouldn't have done that," she stated, tears rolling down her cheeks. He was already weak, like a small child. It happened so fast.

His eyes closed several times. "It was my honor to save you, Liv Beaufont. Forever and ever, I'll watch over you. Wherever I go."

"No!" she cried as her best friend closed his eyes, a sudden stillness in them.

She knew instinctively that he was gone. It was like knowing she would breathe again, or that the sun would rise again.

Sometimes you simply knew another day would come, and sometimes you knew it wouldn't.

Liv Beaufont knew Plato was gone, and there was nothing she could do to bring him back.

CHAPTER TWENTY-SIX

The door at the top of the stairs opened, a glowing light filling the darkened cellar. Liv thought for a moment that Amity had come to check on her before she tucked in for the night. Never before had she been so grateful that others went to bed early.

Her vision blurred as a figure appeared in the doorway. It wasn't Amity's, though. She blinked, and when she could see properly, she recognized the familiar face of Subner.

"Warrior Beaufont, are you all right?" the gnome asked.

Liv tried to stand as she held her dead best friend in her hands. "No. It's Plato. He's dead."

Subner nodded. "Yes, but are you all right?"

She couldn't understand the question. How could she be all right? Plato was gone. Forever.

The gnome sighed. "I guess if you're looking up at me, you have survived, which was all that mattered. I'll teleport you home."

Liv couldn't understand his logic. How was it okay for

her to live when Plato, one of the most incredible creatures to ever exist, was gone from this world forever?

She was about to argue when the emotion and injuries stole her consciousness, sending her into a world of blackness.

She fell into dreams that were closer to nightmares.

CHAPTER TWENTY-SEVEN

The buzz of a saw drilled into Liv's brain, waking her from the strangest dream. She was being chased by a dog. Plato had risked his last life to save her and he'd won, overpowering the hound and surviving. But the simple act of her witnessing his magic stole one of his lives—his very last.

Liv awoke with a start, gasping for air as the nightmare ran across her mind's eye. The scene around her took a moment to compute. The sound of the drill was louder now that she was awake. She recognized the ceiling above her and the unique smell of metals in the air. What she didn't understand was why she was in Subner's shop, the Fantastical Armory.

And then the worst occurred to her.

Liv bolted upright, wondering why it didn't cause her any pain. She thought her ribs were broken, and that she had other injuries. Maybe the dream hadn't been real? Maybe she'd simply fallen asleep on the floor of the shop for some strange reason?

Subner peeked over the counter at her with a curious expression on his face. "And you awoke right on time."

"What?" she asked, pushing upright but finding her world fuzzy all of a sudden. Everything in the shop seemed to sway before it decided to stay still.

Subner was sitting on his usual stool and working at the counter with a drill of some sort.

"'What' seems about right," he said, scooting off the seat and disappearing.

Since Liv was used to this, she simply waited until he waddled around the counter and looked up at her.

"How did I get here?" she began, trying to piece together what she could remember. "Where is Plato? Why am I not hurt?"

"Teleport, down below, and I fixed you," he answered matter-of-factly.

Liv's eyes darted to the machine where he'd been working moments prior. "You fixed me?"

The pain she couldn't deal with yet was starting to well up inside her again. She didn't want to think about Plato. Not right then, not in front of Subner. He couldn't see her pain or the intimate loss she'd experience when she allowed herself to.

"Yes, but that's not very interesting, to be quite honest. Healing others comes naturally to me due to my association with Papa Creola. I was authorized to do it in this instance."

"Well," she began, her stomach growling so loudly she nearly jumped, thinking Russ was about to attack her again. "It's interesting to me since I was coughing up blood and couldn't breathe."

"Yes, you had quite a few injuries." He reached into the case beside him and pulled out a plate of chocolate chip cookies, steam rising off them. "I don't have any milk. You will have to eat these dry."

Liv blinked at the gnome. "You just pulled hot, fresh cookies from a display case but you can't conjure up some milk to go with them?"

He shrugged. "I'm not great with cold foods. It's a gnome thing. We are better with fire and such."

"Thanks," Liv said, feeling like her heart was beating on the outside of her chest. All she wanted to do was throw herself on her bed and grieve for the lynx she now realized was really dead. Instead, she sat back down on the cot and crammed a cookie into her mouth, swallowing it before she'd chewed properly. They were the best things she'd ever tasted, and she wanted no part of that. Right then, she just wanted her strength back so she could portal home.

To her surprise, Subner took the seat next to her, offering an almost sensitive expression.

"You think he's dead, don't you?" he asked, his tone calm.

Liv stopped chewing in mid-chomp. Held her breath for a moment. "Isn't he?"

"Technically."

Liv slid the plate to the side, doing her best to control her emotions. "Talk, Subner."

"Well, in most instances, there is nothing that could bring Plato back after losing his last life," he began to explain. "However, if someone had the foresight to know the lynx was running out of lives, they could plan for such an occasion, but it wouldn't be easy. There are incredibly rare ingredients that would have to be obtained, and it would take a lot of effort, skill, and time to do so."

Liv's heart was pounding so hard in her chest that she was certain Subner could hear it. "Do you mean, like a phoenix feather?"

"As well as a few other things."

Liv suddenly realized that for the first time in a long time, Subner wasn't messing with those metal balls from the giants. "The metal balls?"

He nodded. "As well as a few other things."

"So you were able to save Plato?" Liv asked.

He held up one of his stumpy fingers. "This has never been done before. It's more or less an experiment, and it hasn't worked yet."

"Can I see him? When will you know if it worked?" Liv asked, losing her breath as she talked.

"You can't see him," he stated at once. "Look, I don't know if he'll wake, or if he does, when it will be."

"I don't understand, though. Papa Creola doesn't want anyone coming back from the dead. How could he allow this?"

"He didn't just allow it," Subner stated, pointing at the cookies beside her and encouraging her to continue eating them. "He was the one who gave the order."

Liv picked up a cookie but halted before it reached her mouth. "He *what*?"

"Well, they are his rules, and if anyone is going to break them, it will be him."

"But why?" Liv asked, the cookie still in her hand.

Subner shrugged. "I could hypothesize all day long. However, suffice it to say that Papa Creola has respect for the lynx. Maybe it's a bond based on their longevity, or maybe it's because they share similar magic. All I know for certain is that the Father of Time didn't want the lynx to perish just yet."

"Okay," Liv said, drawing the word out. "Then why send me after Russ? Why not keep him from getting woken up, or kill him before he was a problem, or save Plato from losing the ninety-nine lives before this last one?"

Subner's face remained stony. "Sometimes things have to happen."

"Really?" Liv questioned. "So we went to great lengths to bring Plato back instead of simply keeping him from dying?"

She didn't understand this at all.

"It's true," he answered. "I've been actually working on finding the ingredients for this experiment for quite some time, preparing for this. You see, we can't stop bad things from happening. Papa Creola understands this better than anyone. All we can do is prepare for the worst when it happens, which is what I've been doing. It was inevitable that Plato was going to run out of lives sooner or later. No one truly lives forever, not even Papa."

Liv didn't even know where to begin with all this information. She had so many questions. She cleared her throat, which felt like sandpaper. "Well, if Papa Creola didn't want Plato to die, why couldn't he just bring him back himself?" Liv asked.

Subner held up his finger again. "That's a good question. Again, those two are linked by very strong and mysterious magic. I believe that which created Papa also created

Plato, which means that one cannot save the other. New magic had to be created."

"Which was why you collected all those rare and strange ingredients," Liv guessed.

"Yes, I put together things most could never find, which have magical properties that have never been combined." He tilted his head back and forth. "Whether it worked, we won't know for some time. Papa Creola can't see these events, and has asked that you not dwell on that unknown future."

Liv took a frustrated bite of the cookie, still refusing to enjoy its goodness. "Right, because wondering if my best friend will be brought back to life will totally not soak up any of my attention."

"Good," Subner chirped. "Because Papa wants you to focus your time on finding the next Mortal Seven. You've found two, which is satisfactory, but there's an extremely important one out there who needs to be rescued before it's too late. You must put everything you've got into finding this specific one."

"Why?" Liv asked, tilting her head to the side. "Is this person in danger?"

"All the Mortal Seven are in danger," Subner stated. "There's an evil out there that we cannot see. It's probably what awoke Russ, hoping to draw Papa out to protect Plato."

"But there's a specific one who is important? Why? And I thought that if something happened to a Mortal Seven, their role is passed to someone else, right?" Liv asked, wondering why this particular one was so important.

"True, but what happens to the Beaufonts in the House if you die?" Subner asked.

"We lose our family's position as Royals since there is no one to replace me," she answered.

"Exactly," he affirmed. "But the families who make up the Mortal Seven can't simply be replaced. The magic of the Founders picked those families specifically. This might be the most important Mortal Seven you'll need to recover, because if something happens to her, the House can never be fully reinstated."

"Kind of like John," she guessed.

"Well, because of John's association with you, we were certain he'd be recovered. And now that his chimera has been unlocked, he is protected much more than before."

"Yes, but whether it's John or this other Mortal Seven, their time is still limited, and then what happens to the House? As we've learned from Plato, no one lives forever," Liv stated.

He nodded. "No, but life does go on. I believe that if you recover the last remaining member of the Luce family, she will stay protected long enough to add new members to her tree. And as for John, well, the same is true for him."

"Oh," Liv said, getting the gist of his meaning. "And where do I go to find this Mortal Seven who needs to be recovered before it's too late?"

"Where do you go to find anyone?" he asked.

Liv nodded. She should have guessed that this would require a visit to see her favorite brownie. That was how most of her mysterious adventures started.

She stood from the cot again, glancing at the back door that led to the basement where Plato was. It was hard to walk past there and not see him. She halted, turning back to Subner. "Did you say that even Papa Creola wouldn't live forever?"

A melancholy expression crossed his face. "It is true."

"But if something happens to him, we're all in trouble," Liv said, her voice aching suddenly.

"That's true as well. We believe someone is out there who wants him gone for good. If that happened, it would upset the balance of time for all eternity."

Liv lowered her chin. "Should I explain to you the irony of your last statement?"

He shook his head. "However, one day, Papa Creola's time in his current form will come to an end, and he'll have to replace himself."

"Like the phoenix?" Liv asked.

"That's right," Subner affirmed. "Papa Creola has taken many forms since the dawning of time, and he will take many more. He is always the same and yet always different. The same powers reside in him no matter his form, and yet he changes. So do I and this shop and many other things."

"So he's like a Time Lord, and you're his companion, and the shop is his Tardis?" Liv asked, grateful for the small laugh that fell from her mouth. It wasn't long or hard, but it cut through some of the pain in her heart.

Subner shook his head, giving her a punishing glare. "No, we aren't at all... Well, maybe. Although I'm not sure I like the label 'companion.'"

She smiled. "Oh, I don't know, Subner. I think everyone would want to be Father Time's right-hand man, and he's chosen you. That's pretty cool if you ask me."

The gnome thought about that for a moment and then

nodded, softening slightly. "I guess when you put it that way, it *is* kind of cool."

"Hey, maybe in your next form, you'll be a fae and have ice magic. Then you can serve me milk with my cookies."

He grimaced. "Let's hope the world ends before I'm reincarnated into a fae. I'm not sure I could handle it."

"Well, on that note, I'm going to get out of here. I have a Mortal Seven to save, and I'd prefer that the world not end in my lifetime." Liv grabbed Bellator from the counter. It had been cleaned and was nestled on velvet, appearing ready for the next battle.

CHAPTER TWENTY-EIGHT

It was hard for Liv to focus as she entered the official brownie office. She kept thinking about Plato and all the uncertainty that surrounded him. Before that day, she hadn't known what his secret was and had worried that he had betrayed her somehow, not that it seemed like something Plato would ever do.

However, he had said that he thought she'd be mad at him after learning the secret. He was right. He'd lost probably a dozen lives because of her. It was her fault, and he should have told her never to look at him when he shifted to reveal part of his secrets. But she *had* known that in the cellar with Russ, and she still hadn't been successful at not looking at Plato when he turned into a lion.

Worry filled her head. She wondered if Subner and Papa Creola would be successful at bringing Plato back. And if they were, would he be the same? It seemed that they were defying laws and the odds and risking so much for this. Liv couldn't think of a better reason to do so.

She shook off the fear that bounced around her insides,

trying to monopolize her thoughts. There was nothing she could do for Plato right then. She had a job to do, and that was exactly what he'd want her to focus her energy upon.

Mortimer spun when Liv entered his office. He had a large pair of sunglasses on his face, and he was wearing tie-dye shorts, a Hawaiian shirt, and sunblock on the end of his nose. "Warrior Beaufont for the House of Fourteen!" he rejoiced, clapping his hands. "You're right on time."

"To stop you from wearing those shorts?" Liv asked, putting her hand to her forehead with relief. "Thank goodness. I wouldn't forgive myself if I allowed you to wear something hippies made."

Mortimer laughed. "Already saving me. I had thought these were a bad choice but didn't know for sure." He snapped his fingers, and a much more modest pair of black shorts replaced what he had been wearing on his lower half.

Liv was grateful she hadn't offended the brownie with her joke. She definitely wasn't in a position to give fashion advice, but she also knew that few should wear tie-dye. Really just those who worked in shops that sold crystals and hemp bracelets and children.

"Pricilla is getting Ticker ready," Mortimer informed her. "They will be here in just a minute."

Liv nodded, not connecting why he was telling her this. In truth, she hadn't met the couple's child yet, since the little brownie was always sleeping when she stopped by.

"Now," Mortimer said, piling supplies like books, binoculars, and beach towels into a bag. "I believe you are here to locate another Mortal Seven, is that correct?"

"Yes, that's right," Liv said, always grateful for how easy it was to work with Mortimer.

"I think I've found the next one you should go after. She's been attacked several times by a figure my brownies haven't seen clearly, but thankfully has gotten away each time."

Liv sighed. "That's good news, but I wonder who is going after the Mortal Seven?" she said, mostly to herself. Kayla Sinclair was gone. There was obviously someone else, but Liv had no clue who that could be, and discovering it right then would have to wait. She needed to find this specific Mortal Seven before it was too late.

Still packing, Mortimer said, "I'm not sure. I wish I could help you. However, I can tell you the location of this particular Mortal Seven. She's pretty fierce, though, so be careful. She might think you're one of the bad guys trying to hurt her."

Liv nodded. "Good point. Thank you."

Mortimer patted his shirt pocket. "Now, what did I do with the Mortal Seven's location? Oh, that's right. Ticker has it."

Liv was about to ask why Mortimer would give that to his son when Pricilla entered with the little guy in tow. He was fairly cute, with a round face and elfin ears. On his head, he wore a hat with a long pointy end, like Santa Claus. Ticker had grown a lot and was actually half of Pricilla's size, about a foot tall.

Before Liv could protest, Pricilla placed the little guy in Liv's hands. Her eyes widened, and she held the child out like he was a delicate heirloom.

"Ummm…thanks?" Liv said, looking between Ticker's smiling face and his mother's.

"Thank *you*," Pricilla said. "You're so kind to watch Ticker while we're on vacation."

"Oh, right," Liv said, remembering the strange agreement she'd unknowingly made with Mortimer at their last meeting.

"Aren't you worried about him being with me?" Liv asked. "I do have an important mission that I'm going on, and it can't be delayed."

Pricilla waved her off. "Don't be silly. You're Warrior Beaufont for the House of Fourteen. He's much safer with you than with us."

"I'm not sure about that. When I'm on a mission, it will be hard for me to watch the little tyke," Liv argued, turning to Mortimer. "And like you said, someone is after this Mortal Seven. I wouldn't want to put Ticker in danger."

He shook his head. "Whatever wants this Mortal Seven won't care about my son. Remember that for most, we go unnoticed. Most magicians don't even notice us. And I daresay Ticker might be of help to you."

"Yeah, he might," Liv said carefully, still holding the child at arm's length.

"I know it will be a help to us," Pricilla said, rubbing her stomach. "We could really use some alone time before the next baby comes."

Mortimer beamed at her. "Yes, thank you, Warrior Beaufont. There is no one else we'd trust with Ticker."

So no pressure, right? Liv thought, looking at the laughing child in her arms. Brownie children definitely matured faster than humans, since Ticker was only a few weeks old but appeared very coherent as he watched her.

He thrust one of his fists forward, nearly punching Liv in the nose. In it was a roll of parchment. "Sortal Meven."

Liv smiled meekly at the child and took the scroll. "Thank you."

CHAPTER TWENTY-NINE

Ticker hadn't been nervous about stepping through the portal. Instead, he'd cheered the entire time, yelling, "Nortal Pow! Nortal Pow!"

Liv felt like she needed to sit down with the little brownie at some point and explain language, but he actually seemed to be doing better than King Rudolf Sweetwater, so he was probably fine.

Liv found it strange that she went from having Plato as a companion to an infant brownie. Life wasn't ironic. It was as if the Big Magician in the sky was laughing at her. She thought he or she definitely was.

After refashioning her cape into a carrier for Ticker, she dropped the little guy into it and tied him snugly to her back. He held onto her neck tightly as she strode forward, talking into her ears about the things he saw.

"Wuy galking," he said, pointing to a guy who was striding down the street.

The guy, as Mortimer had mentioned, didn't notice

Ticker on her back. Apparently, even though mortals could see magic, brownies were still quite elusive since that was part of their job—to sweep in at night and clean up a house, going unnoticed. John had mentioned seeing the brownies that cleaned his shop, and even Ireland recalled noticing them a time or two in the bookstore. However, most mortals wouldn't notice a brownie if they slapped them in the face with a dustpan, not that sweet little brownies would ever do such a thing.

"Guy walking," she corrected. "And I don't think he's anything to worry about."

"Hot nim," Ticker whispered into her ear. "Gther oirl."

Liv halted, not seeing a girl, only a punk-looking kid with stark white hair, short on one side and long on the other. She glanced at the piece of parchment Mortimer had given her. It read:

Cassie Luce

Glenrowan, North East Victoria, Australia

That was where she was, walking down what she guessed was the main street. However, Liv didn't know where to look specifically for this Cassie Luce. She kept searching for a dog, a cat, or even a kangaroo who could be this Mortal Seven's chimera.

She spotted a few animals, but they didn't fit the description Mortimer had given her for Cassie. If she was feisty, then her chimera should be too, or at least Liv thought so.

Tourists, passing through off the Hume Freeway with tiny dogs didn't seem like the feisty type. Old women walking chihuahuas were definitely not that type, she thought. And then there was a woman who had a boa constrictor hanging around her neck. That woman hadn't given off a feisty vibe. Scary was more like it.

A bug buzzed past Liv's face, nearly making her jump back. She'd once heard that many of the most dangerous creatures in the world called Australia home. It was hard for her to believe she'd recently faced off with a three-headed dog, but something small with wings nearly made her jump out of her skin.

"Thight rere," Ticker said, pointing adamantly at a beautiful woman in her mid-twenties with long, silky brown hair and a careful smile that she flashed at passersby.

Liv looked back at the brownie and then the mortal who seemed to notice him. She'd done a double-take upon seeing Liv. Now she was definitely staring, a studious expression on her face.

"Excuse me, do you see him?" she dared to ask the girl, pointing to Ticker on her back, her hopes lifting that this might be her Mortal Seven. However, the woman didn't have any pet that she could see, which wasn't a good sign.

The stranger searched Liv and then Ticker and shook her head, backing away. "I don't know what you want. I can't help you. I told your friend to leave me alone."

"Friend?" Liv asked. "I don't know what you mean."

"Just stop following me, or else!" the woman yelled.

That seemed about right, based on everything Liv had learned about this Mortal Seven. She'd been hunted, so she'd be skittish. And if she could see Ticker, that meant she...

"Look, do you see him?" Liv asked, indicating Ticker again. "I just need to know."

That apparently was the wrong approach.

The mortal pulled back immediately, taking a fighting stance. "Just leave me alone. I don't want anything to do with your weird baby or your albino friend."

Albino friend? Liv wondered, all the information suddenly starting to compute. Kayla. The Sinclairs. The deception. Could it be possible? Was Kayla not dead? Or was there another Sinclair who had taken her place?

"Hey, these people after you," Liv said in a rush, "I can help you get away from them."

"No, we don't need your help," the woman said, backing away.

"We?" Liv questioned, looking around. There were a few people standing on a porch beside a large statue of a bushranger covered in metal and holding a rifle, watching her. Ned Kelly, Liv thought, trying to remember her Australian history.

"I'm here to help you," Liv continued, reading the tension in the woman's eyes.

"Then why have you been trying to kill me?" she retorted.

Before Liv could argue or unleash a spell on the woman to keep her from fleeing, she sprinted toward a nearby parking lot. The dust the woman kicked up as she ran made it hard to determine what she was doing. Liv only realized she'd jumped onto a dirt bike when it was too late.

Throwing her foot down hard on the kickstand, the woman turned the throttle and took off. Her engine filling the air with noise as she sped down the road, leaving Liv gaping at the cloud of dust in her wake.

"Sortal Meven."

Liv nodded. "Yeah, I got it. Thanks."

CHAPTER THIRTY

So someone had been stalking Cassie Luce and trying to kill her. That seemed about right, based on the other Mortal Sevens Liv had found. But what she couldn't figure out was where the woman's chimera was. Cassie hadn't been trailed by a large dog or had a parrot hanging out on her shoulder.

Maybe this had all been a mistake. Maybe this woman wasn't the Mortal Seven, and everything had been a coincidence? As the sound of the motorbike got fainter, Liv considered her options. The crowd on the porch was still watching her, but mostly their attention was on a horse trailer being unloaded. The most adorable miniature horses were proudly trotting out of the trailer. Then, out of the corner of her eye, she caught a figure with an unmistakable appearance.

Liv spun to find Kayla Sinclair racing for an open truck. Its owner appeared to have stepped out for a minute, leaving the engine running. With her white hair flying in the wind, the girl sprinted for the vehicle.

Liv lifted her hand to throw a spell at Kayla and stop her progress, but she was already a step ahead. The evil Sinclair threw her hand over her shoulder as she slid into the truck and a bolt of red light flew in Liv's direction.

She wouldn't have been able to avoid the attack and probably would have been blown off her feet. However, a wooden cart stationed nearby jumped in front of her, taking the brunt of the attack.

Whipping her head around, she glanced at Ticker. "Was that you?"

"Mes ye!" he exclaimed.

"I'll take that as a yes," she said, shielding her face and Ticker as wood debris flew overhead. She pointed her finger at the truck, but there were too many mortals close by who might get caught in the crossfire. She hesitated too long, giving Kayla a chance to turn the truck around, its owner yelling and racing out of a nearby store.

Liv glanced around, considering her options. She pointed at the statue of Ned Kelly and muttered an incantation. The figure came alive suddenly, aiming its shotgun from way up high. He fired at the truck speeding away, making it swerve in the road as the bullets hit the back fender.

Again he fired, but this time missed entirely.

That hadn't worked. Liv needed to chase her. Whether Kayla was following Cassie or an innocent person she thought was a Mortal Seven, Liv had to intervene. She couldn't allow this woman to be hurt at the hands of another treacherous and greedy Sinclair.

She looked around for another vehicle. The only one in sight was hitched to the horse truck, and standing around it, quite restless from the commotion, were a few of the adorable miniature horses.

"I don't think that will work," Liv said. She was small, but not that small. Then, from behind the trailer marched a regal and gigantic Clydesdale.

"Bingo!" Liv exclaimed.

"Not name," Ticker stated as Liv ran for the horse, which thankfully was tacked up for riding.

"That was actually correct," she called to the brownie. "And call the horse whatever you'd like. I'm calling it my getaway ride."

The ranchers unloading the miniature horses didn't notice Liv until she'd jumped and thrown one leg over the side of the horse, grabbing the reins for support.

"Hey! You can't do that!" one of them yelled.

"Sorry, I have to," Liv replied, slapping the reins on its haunch and making the Clydesdale take off. "I'll bring him right back. Promise."

The rancher slowed as the horse kicked up dust, making it impossible to follow. The horse was fast, but it couldn't keep up with a truck. Thankfully, from the fluid on the ground, the vehicle appeared to have sprung a leak, making it easier to follow, and hopefully slowing it down at some point.

CHAPTER THIRTY-ONE

C assie Luce zipped the motorbike her grandfather had given her around a sharp corner, taking a back road no one knew about. Just locals. She'd wanted to continue home, but didn't want to lead those two deranged stalkers to her sanctuary.

Ever since the disappearance of every single person in her family, Cassie hadn't taken chances. Yes, she'd rather be sitting on her front porch, drinking a hot cup of cocoa, but long gone were the times she could afford such luxuries. For the last year, it had been only her and Freya. She didn't know what had happened to her parents, her cousins, or her grandparents, but something told her that it had everything to do with the creeps following her presently.

A screech of tires sent a wave of panic through her chest.

She'd been followed.

"Dammit!" she exclaimed, peeling around a bend and immediately taking the bike off-road, zigzagging through the overgrown forest. She stood now to soften the bumps of the uneven terrain, allowing the bike to take the impact.

Cassie knew these trails better than anyone, having been raised out there in the bush. The house where she'd been born was only a ten-minute ride through the bush. Once she was sure she wasn't being followed anymore, she'd hightail it in that direction. Tomorrow she'd pack and head out farther, leaving behind everything she'd ever known—at least for a little while.

Her mother had talked about a place where the fairies guarded their family—The Luces. She'd told her to go there if things ever got too dangerous. That was right before she disappeared, the last remaining family member she had left.

Cassie had always thought her mum was making up the stories about the fairies, but now she wasn't so sure. She couldn't deny all the other strange things she'd seen all her life: gnomes, giants, unicorns, and other strange creatures. Why couldn't fairies be real? And if they were, she hoped with all her being that they really would protect her.

She needed help. It had taken her this long to finally admit that. One could only go so long without sleeping properly, constantly running, checking over her shoulder and fighting to survive.

Knowing that no one was ever on the road coming up ahead, Cassie yanked the handlebars to the side and turned onto the dirt road. Something thundered behind her, and she dared to look over her shoulder.

The road wasn't abandoned as usual. Timothy Punter's ute was speeding behind her, except he wasn't driving it.

The girl with the white hair was behind the wheel, her

eyes crazed as she muttered like she was talking to herself. Not only could Cassie not lead this crazy person to her home, but she also had zero chance of getting away on the open road.

Most would have thought the terrain in front of her all looked the same, but Cassie knew every tree and hill as if it were the markings on Freya's wings. She had studied both for most of her life.

When she passed the tree with a knobby bottom, she jerked the bike to the side, nearly wiping out. Thankfully, she'd done that so fast the ute didn't have a chance to follow her onto the new road. However, a quick glance over her shoulder told her the lunatic was slowing down and turning around.

Cassie was running out of options. The road she'd taken dead-ended up ahead. Worse than that, the forest around her was too thick for her to maneuver quickly on the bike. With the squeal of the engine and getting tangled up every few seconds, she'd be a sitting duck.

What she needed to do was hide.

Before the ute veered onto the road, following her, Cassie turned off the engine and walked the bike behind a cluster of trees. She covered it from view the best she could and ducked down behind it.

Right on cue, Freya flew out of the compartment on the front that Cassie had built for her. The dragonfly buzzed around her head before hovering and landing on her knee. Freya's black and white wings fluttered only once before going completely still as the sound of the ute's tires crunching on gravel sounded just beside them.

Cassie held her breath, counting back from ten. When

she was to zero, she'd jump on her bike and go back the way she'd come. That might give her enough time to get away. By about that point, the crazy white-haired girl would have figured out it was a dead end and turned around again.

"Ten, nine, eight," Cassie said to herself.

Sometimes she wished Freya could speak, if for no other reason than to give her someone to actually talk to. With everyone gone, she'd gotten quite lonely. What she wouldn't give to have someone who understood all the strange things that had happened in her life. To understand that she felt bigger than she was. Someone who knew what it was like to feel the weight of the world on their shoulders for no apparent reason except that her instincts told her every choice she made had bigger implications. That was why she'd resigned herself to the fact that she was crazy.

"I'm just a strange girl living in the middle of nowhere. I'm no big deal," she whispered to herself and Freya as the ute got farther away. "Seven, six, five."

Sometimes she thought Freya understood her. It had been like that since the beginning, shortly after her grandfather had disappeared. She and her mother had been driving down the road. She looked out the window, and beside the car was Freya, speeding along as if trying to keep up with the car. When she'd gotten home, she expected that the strange dragonfly would leave, but she never did. During all these years, when everyone went missing one by one, Freya had stayed. She was all Cassie had left.

The girl smiled at her best friend fondly. "Four, three, two, one."

As quietly as she could, Cassie stood, taking her bike out of its hiding place. With one last glance over her shoulder, she hopped onto the bike and headed back to the main road, Freya safe in her compartment, the wind grazing past her wings.

All Cassie wanted was for this to be over.

She let out a sigh as the ute careened down the road behind her, having apparently turned around. It barreled in her direction.

Actually, not only did she want this to be over, but Cassie also wanted a place where she felt protected for the rest of her life. She hoped the place with the fairies was real.

She prayed it was.

CHAPTER THIRTY-TWO

L iv felt like a complete idiot.

She was racing down a road in the Australian bush on the back of a Clydesdale horse with a baby brownie tied to her back.

In her time as a Warrior for the House of Fourteen, she'd done some crazy things. She'd been in some strange circumstances, but never, ever anything like this.

And worse than her impossible situation was that she'd lost sight of Kayla and Cassie. This shouldn't have been that surprising to her since one of them was on a motor-bike and the other was in a truck, and Liv had chosen the Clydesdale horse.

Thankfully, the horse was very cooperative, especially since she really had no clue what she was doing. However, from her back, she could hear Ticker whispering rapidly. Liv didn't know if this had anything to do with the fact that whatever or wherever she wanted the horse to go, he did. However, at this point, when she'd lost almost every single advantage she had, she was glad to accept this small win.

Everything was riding on Liv finding this Mortal Seven. Cassie was the last Luce in her family. If something happened to her, it could break the House of Fourteen in half for the rest of eternity. Liv couldn't allow that to happen.

However, she had no idea how Kayla was alive. Liv had pushed her off the top of that building in London. There had been reports of a woman's death on the road below.

But those same eyes had seen Kayla Sinclair in Glenrowan, dashing into a truck. And she was a Sinclair, Liv reasoned they were about like Plato and seemed to have multiple lives.

The thought of her best friend and his unknown fate made a gentle sob float to the surface. Liv knew she couldn't be weakened by worry right then, so she shook it off, focusing on the dusty road up ahead.

To her astonishment, the blue motorbike zipped around a corner, speeding in the opposite direction in front of her. Liv's heart leapt with relief; she thought she was close to saving this Mortal Seven from danger. And then the old beat-up truck Kayla had stolen swerved around the same corner, following closely behind.

Liv rolled her eyes, realizing she should have expected this turn of events.

One step forward, three steps back. Always.

She bore down on the horse, encouraging it to run faster.

"Gaster fo! Gaster fo!" Ticker cheered from her back in his squeaky little voice.

Liv couldn't help but smile at the sweet little guy's chanting, and to her surprise, the horse sped up, gaining on the truck.

The ground seemed to melt under the horse's hooves as it sailed across the dirt road, easily swerving past the cloud of rocks and dust the truck launched in their direction.

Liv could see the bike just ahead, its driver frantically looking over her shoulder. Liv knew that expression. Cassie was running out of options. She was scared. Tired of running.

Liv had been there too many times to count, and she didn't want this girl to go through this any longer.

She pulled the horse closer to the truck, surprised at how fast she'd made up the distance.

In the rearview mirror, she could see Kayla's long face. But thankfully, the magician hadn't noticed her yet. She appeared to be quickly repeating an incantation, which worried Liv quite a bit. That might be how she was tracking Cassie, or it could be how she was going to wipe her out. Everything hinged on unpredictable circum-stances at that point.

When the truck was just beside them, Liv reached onto her back and pulled Ticker free. "You stay here. Follow at a distance. It isn't safe for you to go with me."

The little guy nodded. "He melp."

"I know you will," Liv said, giving the brownie a fond smile before fastening him into place on the front of the saddle, ensuring he was safe.

He grabbed the reins, and smoothly, the horse sidled up close enough to the truck that Liv could make a jump unlike any she'd ever attempted.

She gave Ticker one last look before she dove.

CHAPTER THIRTY-THREE

At high speed, Liv jumped from the horse, hurtling over the side of the truck into the bed.

The sudden jolt got Kayla's attention. She glanced up but didn't catch sight of Liv since she'd ducked just in time. Instead, she saw the horse racing beside her and jerked the truck to the side, trying to take out the Clydesdale.

Thankfully, the horse slowed, avoiding being hit. Liv waved to Ticker on the back of the Clydesdale, hoping he'd be okay. Right now, she needed to ensure another innocent soul wasn't harmed.

Rolling over on her stomach, she felt the roar of the engine as the truck picked up speed. The old truck was sputtering and stalling every now and then, definitely pushing it on this leg of the journey.

Liv glanced up, noticing the passenger's side window was down.

When she knew Kayla's attention was on the speeding bike ahead, she made her move. In one swift movement, she launched herself up and to the side, reaching through the open window. Instantly, she heard the chanting. Kayla had been using a tracking spell. Cassie had no chance of getting away from her, no matter how crafty the Mortal Seven was.

However, Kayla was forced to quit chanting when Liv's fingers reached through the car window, scratching at her face. She screamed and swung the steering wheel hard, throwing Liv back. She would have been flung from the vehicle, except that she had a hold of the side of the truck. She flopped down, though, her boots skidded across the road as the truck barreled forward. Kayla continued to wildly jerk the truck back and forth, looking over her shoulder to try to knock Liv loose.

To her delight, she noticed red scratch marks on Kayla's face where she'd attacked her. However, it wasn't enough, and she was currently dragging on the ground, her feet dangerously close to the rear tire.

Pressing her eyes shut, she used an incantation to blast the doors off the truck. A loud screech told her it had worked. She looked up in time to see a metal door soaring through the air and landing on the side of the road. It worked, but to her dismay, she realized it was on the wrong side.

She'd managed to remove the passenger's side door. Funneling her strength, she tried again, not believing that she was having another high-speed vehicular fight. It was laughably ironic.

The distraction had worked, giving her the moment of respite she needed to properly perform the spell. The other door busted off, nearly hitting her it as flew to the side. Thankfully, it missed her and also the horse and

Ticker, who were keeping up with the truck, but not too close.

Liv hoisted herself up, trying three times to kick her legs into the cab of the truck. Kayla slapped at her, trying to steer the truck and also send attacks her way.

To Liv's relief, it appeared that Kayla had used a good bit of her magical reserves to track Cassie.

Liv finally was able to secure her boot on the side of the truck. The other one was still dangerously dragging, constantly knocking into the road. However, this was still going according to plan for Liv. Well, the impromptu plan she had come up with seconds prior.

Putting her weight onto the foot jammed onto the door frame, Liv pushed herself up on her hands, doing a strange backbend and launching her dragging foot straight into Kayla's face, knocking her to the other side of the cab. Blood spattered the windshield when her nose broke.

The truck, without a driver, slowed drastically, swerving back and forth, then veered off the road. Liv was certain they were going to hit a tree they were speeding toward. She let go with her hands, sliding into the open cab and grabbed the wheel. Kayla was hanging out the other side, barely holding onto the seatbelt.

For a split second, Liv felt bad about this. Then she looked into the soulless eyes of the person she was fighting and all remorse disappeared. Whoever this person was, she was undeserving of her sympathy.

Kayla crawled back in, similar to how Liv had. The evil magician launched a fist at her face. Since she was driving, Liv didn't avoid the attack altogether. It was hard enough to keep the truck on the road while also not falling out the open cab. Up ahead, she caught sight of Cassie glancing over her shoulder many times.

The girl had gained considerable distance on them now that the truck had slowed. She could get away if she wanted to. Liv definitely had her hands full at this point.

With strength to impress, Kayla jumped up on her knees on the seat and threw another punch at Liv. She ducked just in time and the girl ended up on her lap. It was definitely awkward since they didn't know each other that well and the girl was pretty much sitting on her, her head hanging out the side.

Liv threw the wheel hard to the right and held onto it for dear life as the truck spun in a three-sixty. Kayla grabbed for her, her legs and feet trying to take hold of something as the sudden movement sent her flying. Liv didn't try to help her. Instead, she used the last of her magical reserves to encourage the girl out of the moving truck and onto the road, where she hit it hard, rolling over several times until she lay flat in the middle.

CHAPTER THIRTY-FOUR

The two crazy people were fighting each other. It was Cassie's chance to flee. To get away. To find the fairies.

She had been watching the fight as safely as she could from the back of the bike. The one girl had ridden up on a horse, and like the bravest warrior she'd ever seen in movies or on television, she'd jumped into Tim's ute and fought the girl with the white hair.

The struggle had been intense. Cassie had nearly crashed as she sped down the road, trying to get away and still see what was happening. It was like they'd used magic. Something had busted the doors off the ute. Cassie had never seen anything quite like it.

And then it had all ended quickly, with the white-haired girl being flung from the ute. The other one, who had long blonde hair, halted the ute, got out, and strode over to the one on the ground.

This was Cassie's chance to get away. She wanted to speed home. Pack. Leave. Escape for good.

But she couldn't understand why the two had fought. Were they fighting over who was going to capture Cassie? Who was going to kill her? She didn't know, and she wasn't sure she should stay to find out, especially because she didn't think she'd survive if the girl with the long blonde hair came after her.

Still, she found herself slowing the bike. She turned it to the side, watching as the girl in black stood over the other one in the road. She lifted a beautiful sword over her head.

Cassie knew what was going to come next. Murder. Death. Things she didn't want to see.

This was her chance to escape. To distance herself from whatever this was that had taken everyone in her family.

Freya peeked out of her compartment, strange wisdom in her round eyes. Cassie knew at that moment exactly what she must do.

She cranked the throttle of her bike as she released the clutch, the gravel crunching under her tires as the bike picked up speed.

CHAPTER THIRTY-FIVE

L iv stopped the truck, checking over her shoulder several times for two important things. She needed Kayla to be there when she halted the truck, and she also needed Ticker to be a safe distance away, although something told her the brownie could handle what had just happened. He wasn't like human children.

To her relief, Ticker had halted the horse a hundred yards away and appeared to be letting it graze on the grass beside the road.

And because somewhere the Magician in the sky was smiling down on Liv, Kayla was lying in the road, not moving.

She needed to ensure that this time, this Sinclair was actually dead.

Swinging her body out of the truck, Liv pulled Bellator from her sheath, carefully approaching the other magician.

Kayla wasn't dead.

Liv knew that by the sound of her ragged breathing and

the fluttering of her eyelids. When Liv stopped in front of her, Kayla brought her chin up.

Liv had never wanted it to come to this, but in truth, that was why she did what she did. The world had evil in it, and if left unchecked, it would run rampant. Her job was to stop it, and that meant doing what had to be done.

She raised Bellator, knowing what she must do next.

"P-p-please," Kayla stammered, choking on blood.

Liv paused but instantly chastised herself for that. She must not listen to the enemy. She was full of lies and deceit. Still, she felt compelled to hear her enemy's last words.

"What?" she growled, wondering what Kayla would beg for now that she was dying.

"P-p-please," Kayla said again, and Liv realized that the magician had something small nestled in her closed fist, lying beside her.

She instantly wondered if she wanted her to do something. To give her something. Maybe make things right. Liv so wanted to believe the best in people, even the Sinclairs.

"What is it?" Liv nearly yelled, holding Bellator at the ready, about to take the final blow. Kayla wouldn't escape her again. Not this time.

To her shock, Kayla smiled, but it looked all wrong on her dying face. "Please die peacefully when he kills you."

Liv had no idea what that meant. She blinked at the girl. She was about to threaten her. Punish her until she got information, but quicker than she should have been able to, Kayla rocketed her hand to her mouth. Liv caught a brief glimpse of a small red pill as it popped into her mouth. A suicide pill.

The girl swallowed. Her head clattered back down to the road.

And then her head slumped to the side as all life left her body.

This time there was no mistaking it.

Kayla Sinclair was dead.

But who was the *he* who would try to kill Liv?

CHAPTER THIRTY-SIX

Liv was so confounded by everything that had happened in the last sixty seconds, she couldn't accurately compute why the girl with long brown hair was speeding up to her on her motorbike on the road.

Disoriented, she glanced between Kayla's dead body and the approaching woman.

Cassie swung the bike to the side, kicking up rocks as she threw her feet down to stabilize the bike. The two studied each other.

Then Cassie's eyes fell on Kayla. "You killed her?"

Liv opened her mouth. Shook her head. Sheathed Bellator. Finally, she said, "No, she killed herself."

Cassie blinked at her, obviously confused. "I saw you two fighting."

Liv nodded.

"Why?" she asked, her hands on the bike like she might take off at any moment if Liv didn't answer the question correctly.

"Because she was trying to kill you," she replied.

"But who am I to you?" Cassie asked. "Why risk your life for me?"

That was a good question.

Liv glanced at Ticker. She thought she could hear the little guy singing. Deciding he was okay, she returned her gaze to Cassie. "You might be one of the most important people I'll have the honor of saving, but after watching you flee today, I think you actually saved yourself."

Cassie pushed the kickstand down and threw her leg over the bike as she stood to her full height. "I've lost everyone I've ever cared about. I want you to tell me what is going on, and I want the truth now."

Liv gave the woman a tender smile, relating to her words. She hadn't lost everyone she cared about, but enough people that she felt this person's pain. "You, Cassie Luce, are one of the Mortal Seven for the House of Fourteen."

The strange expression on Cassie's face told Liv she'd heard of the House. Maybe even the Mortal Seven. It had been on the news lately. However, all she said in response was, "What?"

Liv had expected this. "Some," she indicated Kayla's body, "don't want you where you belong. They will do anything to stop you from taking your rightful position. But it is my job as a Warrior for the House of Fourteen to ensure all the Mortal Seven return, bringing balance to the world of magic."

"Ma-ma-magic?" Cassie stuttered. "So it's true? Fairies are real? There's a place where I'll be safe?" She looked at the woods as if expecting a kingdom to materialize.

"Yes, Cassie. It is real, and it is safe. But it will require something from you."

Cassie took a step toward her bike like it might protect her.

Liv offered her a smile. "The weight of the world will be upon your shoulders."

She shuddered, as if she couldn't believe the words Liv was saying.

"You will have to make decisions that affect many," Liv continued. "As a Mortal Seven, your vote counts twice because we believe you're uncorrupted by magic. Therefore, you'll be asked to preside over matters of supreme importance."

"I don't understand," Cassie said, looking around like the answer was hidden nearby. "How was I chosen? Why?"

"Your family was chosen a very, very long time ago," Liv explained. "I'm sorry you've lost all of them. Someone really bad didn't want the Mortal Seven to come back. You see, once you're in place, the problems that have existed for so long will be no more. When mortals preside over magical affairs, there is balance. There is peace. Some would prefer a world full of chaos."

Liv's eyes drifted to Kayla's body, her mind still confounded by the "he" that the woman spoke of who would come after her. Adler was gone. So was Decar. And Kayla and Spencer. Liv wasn't sure who else could be out there, but she knew with absolute certainty that all of her enemies weren't dead. This person must have been the one who tried to kill Plato, who tried to bring back the SandMan, who was trying to hurt Papa Creola, and who had been thwarting all her efforts since the beginning. It was probably the one who'd had Adler kill her parents. And then, like a puzzle piece falling into place, the words from the hall in the House of Fourteen rang in her mind:

Stop the One and you'll free us all.

Liv knew this had to be the "he." This person was "the One." She wanted to race off to the House and do everything to stop whoever this was, starting with figuring out who he might be. As her eyes searched without seeing, she remembered her current priority. Cassie blinked at her in confusion.

"How are you sure I'm the right person for this job?" Cassie asked.

Liv nodded. "Do you have a pet that has been with you for some time now? A cat? A dog? A turtle?"

Cassie laughed like any of these options were silly. "Yes, but it's strange. You'll think I'm insane."

Liv laughed too. "I think you'll be surprised what all I can digest without batting an eyelash."

Cassie held up her hand, palm down, and whistled, a strange sound that was both low and melodic. From a small compartment on the motorbike, something flew out. Liv had trouble catching sight of it until it landed on the back of Cassie's hand.

It was a beautiful black and white dragonfly, its body curling as it seemed to study Cassie's face.

"Oh, how interesting," Liv exclaimed. She took a step forward, not having expected this.

Cassie reflexively backed away. "What does that mean? You can't take Freya from me."

Liv halted and held up her hands. "I don't intend to.

Freya is what marks you as a Mortal Seven. She, in a way, has chosen you."

Cassie blinked at Liv like she suddenly had something in her eyes. "How do you know that?"

"Because I do," Liv said, feeling the exhaustion tunneling in her brain. "And once I release her, she will protect you for all of your life."

"Release her?" Cassie asked, fear in her voice.

"Release her to her purest form," Liv corrected. "She's a chimera."

A laugh spilled from Cassie's mouth. "No. You mean… There's no way."

Liv loved this part more than any other. "Well, then you won't mind humoring me as I attempt the spell that will release her if all I'm saying is true?"

Cassie shook her head. "I guess, but I have no idea how this tiny little dragonfly—"

Liv had already started the chimera song. She now knew from experience that it didn't take much, and that every chimera "released" at their own speed. That was why she was only slightly surprised when Freya transformed after only a few notes, making Cassie's hand slam to her body as the lion figure materialized. It took up a great deal of space beside her on the road.

"Oh. Dear. God!" Cassie said, taking a step back. Her eyes were wide as she studied the strange serpent tail and the goat head on Freya's back.

"Yes, that was my reaction at first too," Liv replied with a chuckle.

With disbelief heavy in her eyes, Cassie looked back and forth between Liv and Freya. "So this is real?"

Liv nodded. "More real than anything you've ever known in your life." She turned, noticing how good Ticker was being. However, it was past his bedtime, and she'd need to return him home safely soon.

"Do you mind if we go?" Liv asked. "I know this is a lot to take in, but I'm sort of babysitting, and I need to get the little tyke back to his parents."

Cassie's mouth was still gaping open. "My dragonfly isn't a dragonfly."

"Well, technically, your chimera isn't a dragonfly, but she's also kind of both," Liv stated.

"And she'll protect me?" Cassie asked.

"Yes, now that she's been released," Liv answered.

"And I'm going somewhere I'll be safe?"

"Yes, to the House of Fourteen. But first I have to drop off the brownie that's over there on the Clydesdale."

Cassie shook her head. "This is all so strange."

Liv glanced at her wrist like she was wearing a watch. "And it's only Tuesday. Just wait until the weekend."

She conjured a portal, hiding her excitement as the mortal screamed.

"Oh. My. God!" Cassie exclaimed. "What's that?"

"That," Liv said, snapping her fingers, which caused the horse to trot over to her at once, "is what makes traveling in my world painless. Otherwise, most would be dead, since I would have killed them in traffic."

"So I'm really leaving?" Cassie asked, looking around as if trying to take in the bush one last time.

Her chimera shrank back into dragonfly form and landed on her shoulder.

"Yes," Liv stated, taking Ticker off the back of the horse

and cradling the little guy in her arms. She was sort of sad to let him go. He'd been much more helpful than she would have guessed, exactly like his parents always were.

Cassie looked back at her bike. "I don't suppose I could..."

Liv glanced at the bike, reading the fondness in the girl's eyes. "Yes, you can take it."

"Really?" Cassie exclaimed. "There's room for it where I'm going?"

Liv chuckled, thinking no one knew how big the House of Fourteen was since it held so many secrets, its size being only one of them. "Yes, I daresay there will be enough room."

CHAPTER THIRTY-SEVEN

When Liv stepped through the Door of Reflection, she couldn't get the image of Plato's grave out of her mind that she'd just seen. The uncertainty weighed on her more than anything else. It wasn't that she wanted him dead; it was not knowing that was hard. She acutely related to people who had loved ones go missing. They never really knew if they were gone.

At some point, they had to force themselves to grieve for their loss, but in the back of their mind and deep in their hearts, they always held onto a hope that their loved one would walk through the door, explaining why they'd disappeared for all that time.

Knowing the truth allowed the heart to start the process of mending, but currently Liv was living in the place of uncertainty. Still, she'd do it for many years if Plato returned to her one day. Not just returned to her. She had to admit that Plato was important to the world. He had to be, or Papa Creola wouldn't have gone to such extreme lengths to bring him back.

The Councilors all paused when Liv entered the Chamber of the Tree. All the warriors were present too. It was a rare occurrence, and seemed fitting since Liv had the honor of introducing another Mortal Seven.

"Have you found another one?" Clark asked, bolting to his feet, relief and worry on his face as he studied her worn appearance.

Liv knew that he constantly worried about her. Hell, he worried that she'd fallen into a coma if she overslept. It was Clark's job to worry, and he did it better than anyone else. And hers was to throw caution to the wind and dive in head-first.

Taking her place beside Stefan, Liv nodded. "Yes. Cassie Luce will be entering the chamber soon."

Jude stepped out of the shadows, striding over to stand in front of Liv and giving her a strange measured glare. Being face to face with the large white tiger made her insides ache. Was he taunting her, knowing how much she was missing Plato and that he resembled him when he shifted? Or was it something else?

Liv was pretty certain she was losing her mind, even more so than usual when the tiger lifted an eyebrow as if challenging the statements running through her mind. There were so many things she'd considered on the trip there.

The House of Fourteen wasn't safe. There was someone who was betraying them. There was a huge secret she needed to uncover, and since she wasn't sure who could be trusted, it seemed like the right thing to keep some of the information she learned to herself.

"Okay, I'm just going to say what everyone else is thinking," Bianca began with a sigh.

"Why do you always look like you're smelling something putrid?" Liv asked.

That brought Diabolos down from the unseen rafters to take the place beside Jude.

A sound of frustration spilled out Bianca's mouth. "Really, Olivia, this type of behavior is uncalled for."

And there was Liv's first suspect. Of course, Bianca had it out for her. She'd always had her nose straight up Adler's behind, and even after he was gone, she'd continued to be a jerk.

"I realize that remembering things is excruciatingly difficult for you," Liv began in a babytalk voice, "but my name is Liv. Not Olivia. You've been told that many times. Anyway, 'Liv' should be easy for you to remember and spell. It's a capital L and a lowercase—"

"I must agree with Councilor Mantovani," Lorenzo stated, conceit in his voice. "Your behavior really is a distraction to our affairs."

And there was suspect number two, Liv thought. She didn't understand Lorenzo, or why he was working against them on the elf negotiations. Before, she'd figured it came down to pure and awful prejudice, but that was enough of a reason to throw the guy out of the House, if only she could. His sister, Maria Rosario, was also a mystery. She kept to herself and never said much. Maybe that was a good thing. Or maybe it meant they were the spies, working against the House's efforts.

"I think..." Stefan began, a smile in his voice, "Bianca

was referring to the fact that you have a brownie on your back."

Liv turned around, of course not being able to see Ticker hiding in her makeshift carrier. She did several rotations before shrugging like she'd given up. "What? What are you talking about?"

The little brownie giggled, nearly making her laugh too.

Akio, Stefan, and Trudy definitely chuckled, entertained by their antics.

"This is serious!" Bianca yelled, shooting to her feet. "She's brought a-a-a creature that isn't a magician into the House."

"With all due respect," Hester cut in, "it's a brownie. They aren't just harmless, they are extremely helpful."

"I think my question would be how?" Haro asked speculatively.

"I carried him," Liv said matter-of-factly.

She heard Stefan nearly choke on a laugh beside her. Meanwhile, Clark looked like he was about to strangle her and John and Ireland were remaining completely stoic, watching the interactions around them.

"No, I mean, how were you able to bring a creature that isn't a part of the House of Fourteen in here?" Haro asked. "Only Royals should be able to enter."

"Oh, about that," Liv began. "Well, I have a few theories."

"Really, the question should be 'why?'" Bianca asked smugly. "Why did you bring that thing in here?"

"Well, because I had a Mortal Seven with me who I'm not sure is safe on Roya Lane," Liv explained. "And she's pretty new to this world, so I didn't want to plunge her into the chaos that happens at that place right away."

"Why would you have to go to Roya Lane?" Haro asked curiously.

"To return the brownie to his parents," Liv stated.

"Because?" Lorenzo questioned, apparently ready to come unglued.

"Oh, because I was babysitting."

Clark covered his face with his hands. That was a good sign that he was also losing his mind.

"Babysitting? Weren't you supposed to be recovering the Mortal Seven?" Bianca narrowed her eyes at Liv. "Maybe if you spent more time on your job, this wouldn't be taking you so long."

"I did recover some of the Mortal Seven." Liv pointed at John and Ireland. "And I also got them here."

Bianca scowled. "Yes, but I think we can all agree that it's taking you quite some time. Maybe that's because you are messing around."

"Warrior Beaufont, why were you babysitting this brownie?" Raina asked with no judgment in her voice.

"Because his parents asked me to and I owe them many favors," Liv stated. She trusted Raina but couldn't tell everyone that she relied on Mortimer to give her inside information on locations and whatnot. Somewhere there was a spy in the House, and she wasn't giving away anything.

"Well, I think it makes sense that you brought the Mortal Seven straight here," Hester stated. "It would be very confusing for anyone to be exposed to Roya Lane after just being introduced to our world."

"And besides, we had to get her motorbike here safely,"

Liv stated, again matter-of-factly. Right on cue, most of the council's jaws dropped.

"Did you just say 'motorbike?'" Lorenzo questioned.

"Why, yes," Liv answered innocently. "I told the Mortal Seven she could bring it."

Bianca turned to those on the council as if looking for someone to object to this. When no one did, Haro cleared his throat. "You said you had a few theories on why you were able to bring the brownie in here?"

Liv plucked Ticker out of his makeshift carrier and set him down on the stone in front of her. He'd been confined for a little while, and she thought he could use the exercise. Raina and Hester smiled at the brownie as he waddled toward Jude. "Well, he *is* a brownie, and I think they have access to most things."

"Not the House of Fourteen," Lorenzo stated at once. "Only Royals do."

"Right," Liv said, her eyes sliding to Jude. He seemed to be trying to communicate something. "I have reason to believe that..."

The white tiger actually nodded at her. Even if she thought she had been imagining things before, she definitely couldn't dismiss this gesture.

"I have reason to believe that something is controlling and changing the laws of the House, which is allowing things that shouldn't be permitted to happen here," Liv stated, peering at Jude for his reaction. He nodded again. So he did want her to tell the truth.

"And why is that?" Lorenzo asked.

"Well, for starters," Liv began, "Kayla Sinclair's name

was erased from the tree behind you, even though she wasn't dead."

And there it was. The great muttering among the council began, just as Liv had expected.

"You sort of live for these moments where you reveal, don't you?" Stefan asked, a sideways grin on his face.

"It's the only way I get any attention," she stated.

He chuckled. "Right. Because carrying around a baby brownie while wearing road-rash clothes gets you no second glances." He indicated her scuffed boots and pants, which were particularly worn in places from hanging off the side of a speeding truck. She hadn't had a chance to change before entering the House since she had a brownie on her back and a mortal in tow who was pushing a motorbike, followed by a chimera in the form of a dragonfly.

"What happened to you, by the way?" he asked, looking her up and down, more in an appreciative way than with concern.

"Would you believe me if I told you I nearly fell off the side of a moving truck after I jumped from my Clydesdale horse?" Liv asked.

"Again?" he asked in mock disbelief.

She nodded, loving the conversations Stefan and she had. He got her. Or at least, when they talked, she didn't want it to stop, which was rare. Of course, the council had questions, so she refocused on them when they quieted down.

"Are you telling us Kayla Sinclair isn't dead?" Clark asked.

"Well, she wasn't until today. *Now* she's dead-dead," Liv answered.

"How can we be sure?" Haro asked.

"Because I watched her die," Liv stated.

"But you watched her die the first time," Bianca fired back. "So you can understand why your testimony has been discredited."

Liv restrained herself from saying something derogatory, mostly because Ticker was listening as he combed through Jude's hair, making the tiger appear even more regal than usual. "I watched her fall through the fog, then a woman's body was found at the accident scene. I think most would have concluded that the magician was dead. But if it will help, I've had the body sent to the House. You'll find it in your bed, B."

"Oh, really!" Bianca protested.

Haro appeared to be suppressing laughter. "I'm certain Warrior Beaufont is joking. After the ordeal she's been through, it seems she needs to let off some steam."

"Thank you. I do," Liv stated. "Anyway, I know for a fact that she is dead now, and she was again trying to murder the Mortal Seven. She almost succeeded."

"And if the tree dimmed her name," Clark said, slowly leafing through a book, "there is something playing with the rules if she was in fact still alive."

"Exactly," Liv stated confidently.

"But Kayla didn't kill the Mortal Seven for the Luce family?" Hester asked.

"She didn't kill the last one," Liv corrected. "Just like John, Cassie Luce is the last of her family. It appears that someone has been out there ticking off members of the Mortal Seven to prevent them from joining us."

A look of unquestionable grief crossed John's face. Liv knew that much like Cassie, all of his family had mysteriously died over the years. It must have been heartbreaking for him to learn why and be the last one to survive. However, she also believed it made him more eager to do his job as a Mortal Seven.

"Who could be messing with the laws of the House?" Raina asked. "Could there be another Sinclair?"

"Or is it someone among us?" Liv asked, scanning the faces in the chamber.

CHAPTER THIRTY-EIGHT

"Well, Sherlock," Stefan said to Liv over the council's muttering, "is this when you tell us who done it?"

Liv shot him a cold stare. "I know it was you, Ludwig."

He gawked. "I am a lot of things, Warrior Beaufont, but I'm no traitor."

She winked at him. "I know. Otherwise, I would have already killed you."

"I don't doubt you for a minute," he stated, returning the wink.

"How dare she insinuate that one of us is corrupt?" Bianca said, her voice shrill.

"Well, actually, it's the only thing that makes any sense," John chimed in, a solid voice of reason. "Too many events have been going on that would require someone on the inside manipulating the House. I believe it is necessary for us to ascertain that we are all loyal members."

It was strange to see him taking such a role, but it was also completely natural. Liv believed John Carraway to be a true leader. He had only ever needed his moment to shine like he did in the House of Fourteen.

"Actually," Akio said, stepping forward with his hands behind his back, "I believe your chimeras prove that you and Ireland and our new Mortal Seven are trustworthy."

Liv nodded. "That's correct. However, there have been no other checks and balances on the rest of us."

"So what are you proposing?" Lorenzo asked, his tone clipped.

Before Liv could answer, Hester stated, "I think it's obvious. We must all be tested for our trustworthiness."

"And how will we do that?" Bianca asked. "Isn't that the job of Jude and Diabolos?"

"Yes," Liv began slowly, thinking, "but if you remember, they were present when Adler stated many things that were later exposed as lies. Decar, too. And Kayla, who was actually an illusion. So it's possible that the magic that controls them has been tampered with."

"How do we fix them?" Bianca asked, looking down at the animals like they were broken pieces of china.

"I think we have to find out who is breaking the laws, and then we'll know the loophole," Stefan offered, thankfully being a calm voice of reason.

Liv nodded. "I agree. What methods do we have for discerning who is trustworthy?"

"The chimeras," Clark spouted, continuing to flip through the *Forgotten Archives*. "I read something at one point about how the chimeras not only chose the Mortal Sevens who were the most trustworthy, but they could also be used for testing honesty in others."

"Can you research that further, Councilor Beaufont?" Haro asked.

Clark nodded. "Yes, I'll do that, and come up with a process. Then we can all be tested."

"Very good," Hester said, smiling broadly, obviously not having anything to hide.

Liv looked at the faces of the other Councilors, wondering who she could trust and who she needed to kill. She hoped to find out soon.

"Okay, well then, it's probably time that we welcome our newest member," Raina said, her eyes darting to the back of the chamber.

All heads turned to find Cassie standing awkwardly at the back, Freya buzzing around her head.

Liv wasn't sure how long she'd been there listening, but she appeared to mostly be studying the strange space.

Abandoning her spot, Liv strode over to the woman. "Welcome to the House of Fourteen, Cassie. Please come in and join the council."

The Australian paused, hesitation on her face. Liv couldn't blame her after everything she'd been through.

"Don't worry," Liv said encouragingly. "We don't bite. Well, the white tiger does, but it's apparently just a hallucination. Still, it hurts like a bitch."

"And Trudy once bit me when we were on a mission," Stefan added.

The warrior next to him sighed. "I thought you were attacking me."

"No, I'd already killed the snake that did that," he retorted.

The banter of the warriors was new since the Sinclairs

had "left" the House. And it felt right. They were soldiers, but they shouldn't be silenced like in the days when Adler ruled. Also, this seemingly small exchange was enough to relax Cassie slightly, which Liv was grateful for.

"So you all are..." Cassie asked, looking at the sparkling lights overhead and the many faces staring at her.

"We are the Warriors for the House of Fourteen," Akio said proudly.

"And we are the Councilors," Haro added.

"Please join us," John offered, standing with Pickles in his arms.

Liv held out a hand, stopping Cassie. "First, would you do the honors of transforming your chimera? That's how you officially become one of the Councilors."

"Where is her chimera?" Bianca asked, looking around as if searching for a mouse underfoot.

"It's a dragonfly," Cassie answered.

Bianca's eyes widened and she seemed afraid the creature would fly into her hair. "What? Are you certain? That seems highly unlikely."

"I get that understanding magic is difficult," Liv began, "but it makes all sorts of things possible, although I don't think it can get rid of your bad attitude."

Clark shot Liv a look that without a doubt said, "Stop it."

Liv was feeling a bit feistier lately. Nodding to her brother, she turned her attention to Cassie. "Will you please do the honors?"

"What do I do?" Cassie asked, looking at the dragonfly buzzing around her and then Liv.

"Just intend it," Ireland offered.

Cassie nodded. "Okay. Here we go."

A moment later, from seemingly nowhere, a chimera matching the markings of the black and white dragonfly materialized, a soft growl spilling from her mouth.

"Wow! It doesn't matter how many times I see that, it's always beautiful," Hester said, clapping her hands.

"Yes, I agree," Raina said, joining in the enthusiasm.

On the branch of the tree behind the council labeled Luce, the name Cassie was etched into place. Liv smiled broadly as the lights of the chamber intensified for a moment and then dimmed again.

"And now it's done," Liv said, holding a hand out to Cassie and leading her to the bench. "You can take your place on the council. I'd do introductions, but I don't know most of these people's names, so I'm not the right person for that job."

Clark rolled his eyes at Liv as she took her position again. "I'll introduce you to everyone, Cassie. Please have a seat next to me."

As Clark pointed and ran through the names of everyone, Bianca appeared very put out about having the dragonfly buzzing around the bench. It was turning into quite the menagerie, with John's terrier, Ireland's fat cat, and now the dragonfly. Liv liked everything about it. She couldn't wait for the other Mortal Seven to join the council, although it might start to look like a zoo at some point.

"Okay, I think we need to turn our attention to the pressing issue of the elf negotiations now," Haro stated. "We need their support, but they are unwilling to talk to us. With every passing week, we're losing the support of the other races because of this situation."

"I think I have an idea about that," Liv began, earning everyone's attention. "I've recently acquired a position on a board of advisors that also includes high-ranking elf officials."

She was referring to her reluctant willingness to help Rudolf with his new business ventures. When no one asked any follow-up questions, she continued, "I think I can use this opportunity to earn their favor."

"Even though Mr. Ludwig slaughtered many of their enemies to build goodwill and it did no good?" Bianca asked.

"Well, after he did that, Councilor Rosario offended King Dakota Sky and his people, which undermined Stefan's efforts," Liv reasoned.

Many of the Councilors nodded in agreement.

"I really believe," Liv stated slowly, realizing that what she was going to say next might be the most outrageous declaration she'd made to date, "that we must include positions on the council for the other races."

On cue, the council began muttering among themselves, many protesting this idea.

"I'm usually a supporter of your radical ideas," Hester stated. "However, even I have to admit that this is a bit extreme."

"I understand, but—"

"We've only recently brought mortals into the House," Haro argued, cutting her off.

"Actually, mortals were once a part of the House," Liv corrected. "We've only brought them *back*, as they were intended. But if we're going to be a governing body, I think it's only fair that we create positions for the other races.

You see, the problem with the elves isn't their fault. It's ours. We want to police magic, but why are we the ones to tell everyone what they can and can't do?"

"We are the House of Fourteen!" Lorenzo exclaimed. "We were set up for that very thing."

"And that was fine back in the day, when the races were spread out and we mostly presided over our own," Liv countered. "However, we have intermingled, and usually we intervene on affairs related to gnomes, giants, elves, and many other magical creatures."

"I for one agree with Warrior Beaufont," Trudy stated boldly. "I have found it very difficult to earn the respect and adherence to the laws. The gnomes don't trust our system because they weren't part of its construction. The elves think we give special treatment to our own. There are a myriad of problems."

"But we are bound by law," Lorenzo said adamantly, banging his fist on the bench. "We can't just go and change that. The founders stated that we'd be represented by seven magician and seven mortal Councilors and seven Warriors would enforce our rule."

"But what's the point in ruling if no one follows us?" Akio asked, his tone quiet but full of authority.

"As you can see, we're already full and still growing," Raina stated, looking down the long bench. "I'm not one to be opposed to these kind of things, but where are we supposed to put more people? How? I just don't get it."

"It will take some creative problem-solving," Liv stated. "But I suggest we start thinking about how to incorporate the others. If nothing else, we should allow them to have advisory positions on the council. Otherwise, what incentives do they have to follow our rules and laws?"

The council muttered at the conclusion of her words.

"So we change the law," Clark said, continuing to flip through the *Forgotten Archives*. "I've been looking into it, and I think it can be done. I think there are a few ways we can do this succinctly."

"Aren't you already tasked with finding out how to determine if we are all trustworthy?" Lorenzo questioned.

Liv had an idea. "When we are all determined to be trustworthy, or rather I should say, *if* we are, why don't you, Councilor Rosario, take the lead on figuring out how to incorporate the other races into our proceedings?"

The silence that followed her suggestion filled her with dread. She'd hoped to warm Lorenzo up to this idea by making him part of it. He was the biggest opposition to this all.

Finally, it was Bianca who spoke. "When did the Warriors start making suggestions to the council? That's not the way things are designed. You are to take our orders."

"But things are changing." It was Emilio Mantovani who spoke, saying something for the first time that meeting. "I for one think it's overdue. The laws are outdated, not just on who should represent the magical community, but on many other things."

Liv could feel the conviction in Emilio's words. He knew what changing this huge law could do. It would pave the way for changing other laws. For melting away the restrictions that barred him from being with a fae. The rules that kept Warriors from dating. The archaic laws that told everyone how to live their lives. Laws were good if they made sense, but if they were simply meant to control without providing justice, they were doing more harm than good in the long run.

"Emilio, this is not the time—"

"No, I suppose it's not," Emilio cut his sister off. "But soon we will have to review matters that you don't want to, and it starts with this. I think the Warriors should be making suggestions to the council. We are in the field, risking our lives every day. We are the ones who have to fight the resistance of other races because they think we are an overbearing ruling body that doesn't have their best interests at heart."

Liv had never heard Emilio talk this much or so passionately. The chamber remained quiet as he looked at each of the council members in turn before continuing, "And I think someone should take the lead on researching and proposing how we will incorporate other races into the House. Yes, it could be complicated. Yes, it will be messy. But in the end, it will make all our jobs easier if we gain the respect and loyalty of all the other races. And isn't that what we really want?"

No one said a word.

Liv had expected someone to cheer, or unanimous applause. Hester scratched her chin. Raina's brow scrunched. Haro shook his head before saying, "What you say makes sense, but I'm just not sure…"

"Then we vote," Clark stated.

There was no way to argue with that.

"All in favor of looking into ways of changing the laws and incorporating other magical races into the House of

Fourteen, raise their hands," Clark ordered, his hand already in the air.

John, Ireland, and finally Cassie joined him.

"All those who oppose?" Clark stated, dropping his hand.

All the rest of the council raised their hands: Hester, Raina, Bianca, Haro and Lorenzo.

What should have been a victory for the opposition was actually an overwhelming win for those wanting radical change within the House.

"And since the Mortal Seven's votes count twice," Clark stated definitively, "we have more in favor of changing the laws."

"This is ridiculous!" Lorenzo stated.

"No, it's progress," Liv argued. "And no one said the other races *had* to join the council. It is called the House of Fourteen for a reason. But I think allowing them to participate or rule with you over important matters or means of punishments would go a long way toward goodwill. And when we're ready to take that next step, I'm happy to use the relations I'm building with the elves on this advisory board to help. They trust me. They trust Stefan. What we need is for them to trust everyone else in this chamber."

"Since we suggest you take the reins on proposing this law change and plans," Stefan began, "you can design it how you think will work best."

Liv smiled slightly at the guy beside her.

"Yeah, I guess I would prefer to be in charge of something like this. That way it will be done right," Lorenzo stated as the council all began discussing how things could change.

Stefan leaned over to Liv, whispering in her ear, "And if we can get them to change a law as huge as this one…"

She smiled at him, feeling a flutter in her chest. "Then it will be easy to get them to change other laws too that dictate who can be with whom."

CHAPTER THIRTY-NINE

Talon Sinclair was ready to destroy the world.

He thundered across the place he'd thought of as his sanctuary for many long decades. Now it felt like a prison.

He needed to get out. It was time. He couldn't stay inside the confines of the Black Void much longer, not while the council was bowing to warriors and ruining the balance of the House.

Ironically, the God Magician wanted to preserve the world and the way it should be, not destroy it. But what would be the difference when the new blood in the House of Seven ruined all that he'd worked for?

Kicking aside bones, he swept to the far end of the Black Void and back, thinking of all he'd just heard. The Royals knew there was a traitor. Kayla was dead. Despicable mortals were filing into the House, ruining it with their ineptitude. Soon those repugnant magicians would change the laws Talon had carefully constructed to protect magic.

Something had to be done.

Talon was tired of waiting. He actually didn't have anyone else to rely upon. It was up to him now.

He was the very last Sinclair.

And he'd been the first.

He should have known that in the end, it would all come down to him again.

His sunbeam-like eyes swept his chamber as he carefully weighed his options.

Father Time hadn't been drawn out. Each of the God Magician's efforts to end the ruler of time had failed, but that had only been because Talon had to rely upon lesser, incompetent magicians.

It was time that he did things himself. Talon was finally strong enough. Yes, Father Time could come after him. He could stop him. He was the only one. However, if Talon stayed inside the Black Void, it wouldn't matter. The God Magician would lose everything anyway. What was the point of living forever and losing all that he'd worked for? All that he'd always wanted?

He could taste the power he craved. He deserved it. More than anyone.

If the God Magician left the Void, he could take back all the power, ruling the way he was meant to from the beginning.

There was still one enemy he could wake who would buy him some time. She couldn't kill Father Time. However, she could keep him still until Talon could figure out how to do it himself.

CHAPTER FORTY

"Well, I think that went well," Rudolf said proudly as he and Liv strode down the street to Rory's house.

"You puked on the boardroom table," Liv countered, recalling the way the king of the fae had concluded his first meeting with his board of advisors.

"Yes, but that's totally your fault."

Liv found herself looking around, expecting Plato to materialize. Hoping he would. Praying. Finally, she gave her friend an impatient look. "Please tell me how that was my fault. I need to know."

"You didn't tell me not to eat a whole pizza before the meeting," he answered.

"I didn't even know you had eaten a pizza," she replied.

"Well, see, there you go. If you took your job as chief advisor a bit more seriously, you would know. Then you would have said, Almighty King, one pizza is okay, but two is no good."

Liv rubbed her stomach, trying her best to keep her

own lunch down. "You ate two pizzas before your first board meeting?"

"I realize it was a bad idea now," he stated, not at all embarrassed. "Usually one is okay, but two is apparently not smart. I know that now. But other than that, I think things went well."

"The elves have some good ideas," Liv stated, happy she'd earned some credibility with the king of the elves. It would do her good when the time came.

"You know, it could have also been morning sickness, me throwing up on the table," Rudolf stated, as if the idea had just occurred to him.

"Again, you aren't the one who gets sick when Serena gets pregnant, which she isn't yet."

Rudolf nodded. "That's right. But my breasts do get tender, right?"

"Sure," Liv said, rounding the corner and heading down the path to Rory's house.

She was surprised to find Stefan sitting on the steps waiting for her. He looked up, his black hair falling in his face, his blue eyes lighting up at the sight of her.

"What are you doing here?" she asked as he stood.

He extended his hand and a small figurine of a white tiger materialized. "I thought I'd bring a gift for your brownie friend."

Liv smiled and picked up the trinket. "Thank you. That was thoughtful." She and Stefan had returned Ticker to his parents that afternoon. The brownie had talked about the white tiger the entire time, or at least, they'd guessed that was what he was talking about. The little guy kept saying, "Tig biger!"

Rudolf keeled over, grabbing his stomach. "I think the pizza is still trying to make a dramatic exit."

Liv shook her head at the fae. "Go ahead and go in. Rory probably has something to help your stomach, like antacids or an axe."

"An axe would be good," Rudolf said, dragging himself up the stairs. "I'm going to cut off my stomach."

"Good luck," Liv called to him, returning her gaze to Stefan. "Okay, spill it. Why did you actually come here?"

He gave her a guilty expression. "Well, you brought Rudolf. Why can't I come to this momentous occasion too?"

Liv sighed. "It's no big deal."

"Then why did you chew off all your nails?" he asked, not looking down at her fingers, whose nails had been chewed to the quick, but rather maintaining a thoughtful focus on her eyes.

"Look, it's not like Donald has hatched or Sophia is leaving," Liv reasoned.

"No, but it's the beginning of that next chapter, and I think you know that," Stefan stated. "And without your best friend... Well, I just suspected that you could use an extra shoulder."

She lowered her chin and regarded him from hooded eyes. "Shoulder? For what?"

"To punch, obviously."

Liv laughed. It felt good, and broke the tension building in her chest. She held up the figurine. "This was thoughtful. I'm sure Ticker will like it. He'll probably talk about the hemon dunter for a long time."

"I sure hope so," Stefan said with a sigh. "Get in good

with that guy, and I'll be golden for ages. He's from a pretty helpful family."

Of course, Liv had confessed to Stefan that she used Mortimer to find all her leads. He was impressed that she had used such an inconspicuous source. Most bribed influential elves or tried to seduce lonely gnomes, but making friends with brownies was apparently pretty smart—at least according to the demon hunter, which was all that mattered to Liv. She liked that Stefan admired how she handled her business. His approval wasn't necessary, but it felt good. And although she didn't care what most thought, it meant a lot that she cared what he did.

"So, for real," Stefan said, his face suddenly serious. "How are you?"

"Well, I think that when Subner fixed my broken ribs, he stole one. My armor doesn't fit like it used to."

Stefan laughed. Again, not most people's reaction to such an admission. "Well, I'm sure he's going to use it for an important project."

"We can only hope," she said. "But other than that… well, I'm sort of okay."

A pained smiled wisped to his mouth. "And I'm happy you're sort of being honest with me."

Liv shrugged. "Well, what's the point in pretending with each other?"

"There is no point," he stated, leaning close.

Liv felt his breath brush her cheeks. She could feel his warmth. His intensity. It was enough to make her say to hell with the law. She closed her eyes, preparing to fall forward into him.

"Hey, you two," Clark called from too close by.

Liv's eyes sprang open. Her brother and sister were striding down the walkway toward them. "Hey."

"You'll remember the law hasn't changed yet, and you two aren't supposed to be getting along so well," Clark said in a disapproving voice.

"What? We're not getting along," Liv argued.

"Yes, we are," Stefan fired back, gawking at her.

"That's only because you like things that are broken," Liv countered.

To her relief, Stefan laughed, extending a hand to Clark and smiling down at Sophia.

Liv turned her full attention on her little sister, who was wearing a black-and-white-striped dress. She kind of resembled Cassie's beautiful dragonfly.

Liv had stayed with the new Mortal Seven for an hour after the council meeting, but had quickly realized that her adjustment period wouldn't take very long. Cassie had everything she'd wanted for a long time: a place to belong, people who understood her, and protection. Liv had finally left her with Ireland and Harry, who was actually playing quite civilly with Freya.

"Hey, Soph," Liv said sensitively. "Are you ready for this?"

Sophia nodded. "I'm fine. I might not have seen my dragon in a few days, but I'm not sad. I miss him, but I know that until he hatches, this is for the best."

Liv nodded, reading the sincerity in her sister's eyes. This wasn't hard on the little magician, not like it was on Liv. Stefan was right. It was the beginning of the end for Liv. Soon the dragon would hatch and the Elite would know, and Sophia would be gone forever.

The only good news was that moving the egg had hidden the dragon's energy. There hadn't been anymore inquires from the Elite according to Raina and Clark, who had been intercepting all of the correspondence before it reached anyone else on the council. The bad news was that Sophia had to limit her time with the egg for now. This would be her first time to visit him since he'd been moved.

"Okay, lovely lady, shall we go in?" Liv offered Sophia her arm.

"That would be lovely, mademoiselle." Her sister curtsied and took it.

CHAPTER FORTY-ONE

Liv thought the squeal that escaped Sophia's mouth was because the backyard had been entirely transformed, complete with a lava pit and tropical plants. However, when the little girl ran straight over to the large egg, throwing her arms around it, Liv knew the truth.

Those two being apart hurt them. It was apparent in the way Sophia nuzzled her face against the blue shell, like they'd been separated for decades instead of days. And now, from this distance, Liv realized that once again, Sophia had grown rapidly, probably gaining another inch. Soon she'd be as tall as Liv, which wasn't that impressive a feat, but it was all happening so fast.

Rory took the spot next to Liv, not saying anything but rather just staying as close to her as Stefan, Clark and Rudolf were helping Bermuda with a project on the other side of the yard. Liv actually appreciated Rory's quiet presence right then. He seemed to be offering sympathy without saying useless stuff she couldn't do anything with. The two simply watched as Sophia sat next to her egg, talking incessantly, telling him all about what she'd been doing for the last few days.

When Liv's lips pressed together and her chin dimpled from holding in the emotion, Rory said, "How does an accountant stay out of debt?"

Liv turned to the giant, totally taken off-guard by the question. "How?"

"He learns to act his wage," Rory answered, a total deadpan look on his face.

Liv's eyes widened but she quickly covered it with a nonchalant expression. If she overreacted, this might be the last joke that Rory ever told. Instead, she nodded. "Rory David Laurens, you're a good friend."

He shook his head. "That's not my middle name."

She waved him off. "I know that, Rory Steven."

Pointing at the pair cuddled on the island next to the lava river, he said, "They seem to be getting on well."

"Yeah," Liv said, not able to say anymore.

"About Plato…"

Liv sucked in a breath. "You never much cared for him. Don't worry about saying anything."

"I know that a lynx is full of secrets, but not until I heard what you told mum did I fully understand why," Rory said sensitively. "She's really grateful you passed along the information for the book. It will help to fill out that chapter."

"Well, hopefully it helps someone, someday."

"There isn't anyone quite like Plato," Rory stated. "There are other lynxes, but he's different; full of a unique magic, I believe."

Liv nodded. "Apparently…" She wasn't sure what to do

with all this sympathy. It was seeking to destroy her, little by little. She suddenly missed the rib Subner had stolen, and considered leaving to go and get it. Just when she was about to argue with herself that this was an attempt to avoid her emotions, a commotion broke out by the fence.

"I know what I'm doing," Maddie stated, her tone firm.

Bermuda, who was only a nose-width away from her face, clenched her hands by her side. "I think you know how to make barbeque and wait tables, but this is all a bit much for you, dear."

Liv and Rory exchanged vigilant expressions.

"Should we interfere?" Liv asked.

"They do this at least once a day," Rory said with a sigh.

"So they are getting along well, then?"

He shook his head. "No. I think I'm going to have to ask Maddie to leave."

Liv turned to face him. "Do you want her to leave?"

"No."

"Does she want to leave?"

"Well, no," Rory said, shaking his head. "She told me this has been good for her. And she's teaching me all about cooking, and I've been helping her…"

His voice trailed away and he hung his head.

"But Bermuda doesn't like her," Liv stated.

"Mum is just protective," he argued.

"You know it's more than just that."

"I know, but what am I supposed to do?" Rory asked, and for the first time, Liv got the impression that he really wanted her to tell him.

That was the reason she jumped up on a nearby rock, putting her nearly at eye level with the giant. She placed her hands on her hips and said, "Rory, go and fix things. Make Maddie feel at home if she wants to stay, and tell your mum to stop being a bully. If you want something… well, something that's worth fighting for, you're going to have to start standing up for it. Otherwise, there won't be anything to fight for. Bermuda will tell you what to do and you'll do it, and that will be the end of it."

He glanced in the direction of the feud and back at Liv. "But…she'll be mad."

"So?" Liv challenged.

"She can hold a grudge," Rory reasoned.

"*So?*" Liv stated more emphatically.

"But what if—"

"What if you live the rest of your life not doing or being who you want? Will you be happy then?"

"No," he stated, throwing his hands up. Everyone was so focused on the two giants fighting they didn't even notice the exchange Liv and Rory were having.

"And are you happy now?" Liv asked him.

"Well, sometimes," he admitted. "When I'm gardening. Cooking in the kitchen. I like painting. And, well, there's something else I've always loved, but I've been too afraid to tell anyone about it. And then there's Maddie. I like her."

Liv smiled. "Then fight for what you want. You can live the rest of your life being safe, or you can take a chance to have and be who you are. But if you allow other people's standards to dictate the way you live, you might as well lay down and die right now, because you'll have never lived at all."

Rory's mouth pinched and his eyes filled with emotion

as they drifted to the fence where the two were still arguing. Finally, he nodded and marched off toward the feud.

Liv knew she should give the giants some privacy, but she also wanted to warn Clark and the others to back up before the ruckus started. She went to pull them back, but not before Rory stepped in front of Maddie, facing his mum.

"Stop nitpicking her," Rory said, his voice quavering, but only slightly.

"Oh, dear, you don't understand," Bermuda stated. "She was digging the post holes all wrong.

"Then tell her that," Rory stated.

"Really, I shouldn't have to," Bermuda argued. "If she'd been raised on the island, she'd know how to do manual labor. Sure, she can marinate steak, but the girl has no grit."

"Mum, all you do is criticize her. And, well, me too!"

Liv had rarely heard Rory raise his voice. She looked sideways at Stefan, who shared her cautious expression.

"Rory Dustin Laurens, how dare you raise your voice at me?"

"Dustin!" Liv shouted triumphantly, earning the attention of everyone. She cowered into Stefan's shoulder. "Sorry, just happy to know what to put on Rory's next birthday cake."

Rory turned back to his mum. "Maddie is staying here. She likes learning about life here on the West Coast, and I like having her help."

"But honey, she really should go back to Liam," Bermuda argued.

"I don't want to," Maddie interjected.

Bermuda looked over Rory's shoulder. "Of course you

do, honey. You're just confused. It's all the sweating, which you're not used to."

"Mum," Rory urged, regaining her attention. "Let her do what she wants. For that matter, let me."

"What do you mean, son?" The contemptuous tone in the giantess' voice made the hair on Liv's arms stand up.

Rory swallowed. Stood tall. "I don't want to be an accountant anymore."

Bermuda's eyes widened so far that Liv thought they were about to pop out of her skull. "What? How can you say such a thing?"

"Well, I'm saying it because I've felt it for a very long time," Rory explained.

"But your father, and before him—"

Rory shook his head. "I don't care. I don't want the family business. I never did. But you never gave me a chance to tell you what I really like to do."

Bermuda drew in a breath. To Liv's astonishment, her eyes connected with her. There seemed to be an exchange between them. Was the giantess remembering the conversation they'd had while following the moving truck? She cleared her throat. "Rory, what do you want to do?"

He smiled, and it was pure and unabashed. "I really want to be a fiction writer. I always have."

Bermuda swayed. Liv thought she might topple over. Instead, she steadied herself on the fence post. "Fiction writer? Is that a joke, son?"

"No," he stated at once. "I have stories I want to tell. Things that make me feel alive. I don't like numbers, but I love stories. And I like having Maddie here." He turned to the girl at his back. "If you want to stay, you should do it. I enjoy having you to teach me things, and I'm hoping—"

"I want to stay, Rory!" Maddie said, throwing her arms around his shoulders and hugging him tight.

He released her after only a few seconds and turned back to his mum, but it was still progress. "Mum, I don't want you to be mad, but I want you to accept me. And Maddie. And Liv, and—"

"I don't know why you had to throw the magician into this," Bermuda snapped bitterly.

"Because she's my friend and you're hard on her," Rory stated.

"I kind of like it," Liv chimed in, earning an elbow in the ribs from Stefan. "Hey, don't add injury to insult."

He smiled at her. "Let them have their moment."

She winked at him. "Fine, why don't you help me with…" Liv looked around for something to do. Sophia was still chatting excitedly to her egg. Clark and Rudolf had moved off to the kitchen, apparently to eat, like that was a good idea for the fae. There was absolutely nothing for Liv to do for once, and she felt useless and lost because of it. She reasoned that John might need her help at the shop, but then remembered he had Alicia, and the two probably wanted time alone together anyway. Liv sort of wanted that too: time alone with herself for once.

"You know what, I think I'm going to head home," Liv said after checking briefly on Rory and Bermuda. They were hugging, and Maddie hadn't run off. It might take some time, but those three were going to get along.

"Okay. Do you want me to walk with you?" Stefan asked thoughtfully.

Liv shook her head. "No, but please stay and make sure that…" Liv looked around at the friends she loved with all her heart. "Please stay and just have fun. And make sure that all these people that I love also love each other. The best you can, anyway."

"Fine, but that's usually your job," he stated. "I'm not as good at it as you are."

Liv offered him one last smile as she backed for the door. "I trust you to fill my shoes, Ludwig. If anyone can, it is you."

CHAPTER FORTY-TWO

L iv walked all the way home from Rory's on backroads. All twelve miles. She forgot that she was walking half the time, just operating on autopilot.

It wasn't until she was almost to her apartment that she halted suddenly, having a strange déjà vu moment. She turned, feeling a cool wind rolling over her cheeks.

"This is…" She didn't finish her sentence. Not because she couldn't, but because she didn't want to.

The spot where she found herself was exactly where she'd met Plato five years prior. Strangely, it was about the same time of day, based on the pink and orange glow of the sunset. Liv remembered having just lost her parents and thinking she'd never be able to breathe the same way again. She felt that way right now, but differently.

The day she had met Plato, or rather he'd found her, she remembered stepping on a piece of trash. She recalled it right then like it was that morning, clear and crisp in her mind. Wondering what was stuck to the bottom of the only pair of shoes she had, she bent over. When she looked up, the black and white cat was standing just in front of her, having materialized seemingly out of nowhere.

Liv remembered not being startled at all. She had simply smiled at the cat and said, "Hello."

When he'd responded to her, she hadn't even questioned that he was speaking to her. Sure, she'd had strange animals in the House, but not talking cats. Still, when he asked her where she was going and she shrugged and said, "I don't know," she didn't mind telling him about how lost she was.

Then he suggested she go down the block to check it out, and that had led to John's electronics shop and the rest. Well, it had led to the better life she had now. Maybe Plato wasn't meant to be a part of her life forever. He had definitely helped her fix it, though. He'd taken her from that disadvantaged, beyond-heartbroken girl to the warrior who would fight for every single one of her friends. And more shockingly than anything else, she now had friends.

Liv looked up at the sun, streaked with color, and pressed her hands to her chest. "Thank you, Plato."

She half-expected him to materialize and say, "You're welcome, but we're out of toilet paper."

When only the sound of cars honking in traffic greeted her ears, Liv let out a disappointed sigh. She just had to move on. Pretend she'd gotten the coroner's report.

Yes, it was morbid and horrible, but what else was she to do? Continue to look over her shoulder, waiting for him to show up and save the day? There wasn't always a happy ending, and she needed to start preparing for that.

Tomorrow, she had to continue to track down the

Mortal Seven. And then there were the elf negotiations. And more importantly, finding the traitor. She had no time to be distracted. Plato would want her to move on. He had died for her.

Liv swallowed the tension in her throat, deciding she was going to spill every single tear once she got to her apartment. That was what she needed. It was overdue. Tomorrow she'd fight, negotiate, and lead. Tonight, she'd grieve.

She nodded like she'd made up her mind. Took a step forward. Her foot crunched on a piece of trash.

Liv's eyes widened, and she held her breath. Glanced down. Picked up the paper cup stuck to her shoe and braced herself.

She expected to find the black and white cat staring at her when she looked up. She needed him to be there.

And when he wasn't, her heart nearly broke again. She pushed her mouth to the side, keeping the tears at bay.

"It never happens the same way twice," he said from behind her.

Shock overwhelmed her. *It couldn't be real. That voice. And yet it was!*

Liv pressed her hands to her mouth, coughing on the tears. She was simply vibrating with emotion now.

Now that she was focusing, she could feel him. Maybe sitting on a dumpster. Or maybe she was losing her mind. Anything was possible after everything she'd been through.

"I'm here. I'm real," he said when she didn't turn around.

Liv held her breath and turned to find that either she was hallucinating, or dreams really did come true. Sitting on the top of a dumpster was the lynx she'd grown to love and depend on more than she'd ever thought possible. He was different, though. Better, somehow. Younger. Still the same, but whereas before he'd had a few battle scars, he was unmarked by time. Brand new.

"Plato?" Liv asked, needing him to answer to his name.

He bowed his head, blinking at her with his bright green eyes. "At your service once again, Liv Beaufont."

"Y-y-you're back?" Tears now streamed down her cheeks, soaking her shirt, but she didn't care.

"It appears so," he stated. "Most lynxes only get a hundred years, but none have ever belonged to you. You defy the odds."

Liv shook her head. "No, Papa Creola didn't want you to die. You're special, Plato."

He nodded. "I am. Because lynxes are unique. We're rare, and none have ever belonged to anyone, ever. Not until now. I chose you, Liv. I choose you still. I'm not going anywhere. Ever."

He jumped off the top of the dumpster, gracefully sliding against her leg and looking up at her. "You want to head home now? I could use something to eat."

Liv nearly snorted on her tears and laughter. "Sure, but you're cooking. I'm beat."

"How about takeout?" he offered. "I could use something crunchy."

"Like steak nachos?" Liv asked. The tears were still coming, but they were filled with the silly laughter of relief.

"Oh, no. I'm a vegetarian in this lifetime."

Liv halted. "What?"

Plato looked at her, shaking his head. "Oh, come on. I came back from the dead. I'm overdue for a couple of bad jokes."

Liv shook her head in relief. "Yeah, you'll have to tell me all about it. What was it like? Did you meet the Big Guy?"

"If you mean Rory's grandfather, no," Plato answered, striding beside her.

The two continued to walk through the darkening streets, talking about what they would do tomorrow, and the next day, and the next. Liv knew what would ensure she fell asleep peacefully was that there would be a next. Plato had been reborn. Like the Phoenix, he'd risen from the ashes and was ready to live another hundred lifetimes.

They'd need those for the adventures in store for them —but not until tomorrow.

"Can you cover dinner?" Liv asked. "I sort of left my wallet at the House."

"Ummm, brand new body. No wallet. Oh, and I'm a cat."

"Oh, so you can turn into a lion and kill a hellhound, but you can't pick up dinner?" Liv asked.

"Yes, and speaking of which, the reason I never killed Russ was because whoever takes out Cerberus has to replace him," Plato explained.

Liv paused, her eyes wide. "So what? I have to guard the underworld?"

Plato shook his head. "No, I'm technically the one who killed Russ, and then I died."

"So you're leaving again?" Liv asked, fear overwhelming her again.

"No, but tomorrow we need to start looking for Russ's

replacement," Plato explained. "As long as we put someone in his place, we'll be fine."

"But won't they try and come after you, just like Russ?" Liv questioned. "Won't they think you belong with them?"

"Yes, which is why we put them to sleep and lock them up again," Plato stated. "We just need someone to guard the underworld. They don't have to be awake. The best guards are usually asleep."

Liv shook her head. "Okay, nachos tonight. Replacing the guard of the underworld tomorrow."

"Oh, and you need a new sofa," Plato said discreetly.

"What's wrong with my sofa?" she asked.

"When I awoke…from being dead, I was excited and might have shredded it."

Liv nodded. "I guess I get it. I can buy a new sofa."

"And a bed," Plato added.

Liv huffed. "Fine."

"And new pillows."

A pure chuckle full of warmth and relief filled the night air. "Plato, I'm glad you're back. No, not glad. I'm beyond happy. If you allowed such things, I'd hug you."

"Well, maybe later, after I've turned around six times and licked myself for twenty minutes, we can cuddle for a little bit," he allowed.

"That would be nice," Liv said as they rounded the corner out of the alley.

"And remember what I said, Liv." Plato stopped, making her do the same. He appeared so young. Exactly the same as before, but reset in so many ways. "I'd lose another hundred lives for you. We have many battles to fight, and you won't always be able to look away. So the next time you don't, please know it isn't a big deal."

Liv nodded, smiling down at the lynx. "Okay, but use your lives sparingly, because I promise to live a really long time, and I need my best friend with me for the rest of my years."

Plato winked. "I promise. I'm not going anywhere, Liv Beaufont."

What the two had spoken were promises made and sealed between best friends, the strongest spells two could cast. It was an oath in the magical world that fused two souls together for the rest of eternity.

Thank you so much for reading. Seriously! Book 11. I couldn't be here about to write book 12 if you all weren't supporting the series. Thank you.

I've been looking for the perfect nickname for Michael for a long time. He has a lot. Yoda. MA. Manderle. But none of those have the right ring to them. I think I've got the right one. Read on to find out the name that will stick.

First off, a huge thank you to Micky for the awesome idea about the carousel of animals that had been spelled. She threw that out in our Facebook group, LMBPN Ladies. If you haven't, please join it. It's not just ladies. We have some pretty rad guys in there. It's just a name. We discuss all sorts of things. Sometimes I rag on a guy I dated or something of the like, but for the most part, it's just a bunch of awesome readers discussing books and stuff we love.

And that was me getting completely off topic. Anyway, Micky made this suggestion and I totally ran with it in this book. I loved it! So thanks to the awesome JITer, Micky, for being incredibly supportive and creative.

Speaking of awesome readers in the LMBPN group, I had one come to me and offer suggestions for one of the books. Veronica is always offering up fun ideas related to the Australian culture, where she lives.

This time she asked me if I would include her daughter, Cassie, in one of the books. If you've read this far, then you know where I included Cassie in book 11. She became none other than one of the Mortal Seven. It was a blast working with Veronica to learn about the Australian bush, culture, geography and quarks/interests of her daughter. At the end of writing those scenes, I felt that including the inspiration from a reader, actually made the books way better than if I would have come up with my own stuff. I would have never thought to have a girl riding a dirt bike in the books.

Side note, I've never ridden a dirt bike, so guess who had to spend half a day watching YouTube videos on the subject? If you guessed me, then you get a billion points. Good job. They are useless and not an official form of currency. Sorry.

Anyways, as an author, I get a lot of messages from readers. It's always encouraging and inspiring to hear from readers. I can't always include ideas that readers send me because the story really does have to come first. And whether you believe it or not, I don't really control where the story goes most of the time. Actually a ton of the time, I'm surprised by how things turn out. However, when I can include an idea or suggestion, I know that it makes the books that much richer. So join the group, send me your ideas and keep reading. Thank you a ton!

One last thing before I turn you over to Michael. Playlists are really important to me when writing a series. The songs usually reflect different characters in the books or situations they'll encounter. If nothing else, then the music should get me in the right mood.

I listen to the same playlist over and over again, adding to it periodically, while writing the series. Since this is the longest series I've written, the playlist is pretty long for Liv and I've listened to it a ton. I'll be sharing that with you in the next book's author notes.

However, there is one song in particular that absolutely reflects the essence of Liv better than any other in the playlist. I reference it a tiny bit when Liv fixed up the old jukebox for John and filled it with Beatles' music. Anyway, the song is Blackbird.

What do you think? That fits Liv pretty well, huh? "Take these broken wings and learn to fly...All your life. You were only waiting for this moment to be free."

I hope you sang those lines. I can't read them without doing so.

Okay, without further ado, I turn you over to Michael, aka Bird Killer.

P.S. After making the Blackbird reference, that nickname is a lot more sinister...

Leave Liv alone, Bird Killer. :)

MICHAEL'S AUTHOR NOTES
SEPTEMBER 5, 2019

"Birdkiller?" I work with Sarah to produce the ultimate character based on the person she knows better than ANYONE in the world and in the end, I am condensed down into a short compound word that is an effort to sum up my sum total of existence...

I'll get back to you in a moment, Ms. Noffke.

To you, our fans, THANK YOU for reading our stories – we could not do what we do without you.

Now, back to the Shamer.

AKA Liv AKA Noffke, Noffkismet, Noffmeister, ... the Sarah. Yeah, you, SN.

I see what you are, a young woman who likes to hide behind the bluster of life, scared to share with the world who you really are...

Wait, hold on, I'm not sure I can hold a straight face as I type this stuff. Seriously, who is going to believe you are a soft flower waving in the wind of creativity as the breath of ideas break off your petals to float on the wind of ...

Something.

You know, I think I'm too tired to fight anymore with Liv...Sorry, Sarah.

We have one more wonderful book in the series, and I am admitting defeat in the 11th round. Next book, I'll make up some incredible lies about Sarah, and she will have to always wonder how I meant them.

BWAHAHAHAHAHA!

(Totally not giving up, PSYCHE!)

ACKNOWLEDGMENTS
SARAH NOFFKE

My favorite part of writing any book is creating the acknowledgements page. It reminds me that writing a book is not a solo task. I might sit alone and write, but the finished product is a result of the support and encouragement of a tribe of people.

Thank you to the readers who buy the books, read them, review and recommend. YOU are the one who keeps us writing. I'm always inspired by the messages I receive from readers. Thank you supporting the books and offering so much richness to my life.

Thank you to my LBMPN family for all the support. Steve, Michael, Lynne, Moonchild, Jennifer and so many others who help champion the book to publication and beyond.

Thank you to the beta readers who offered so many valuable insights early on. Thank you to John, Chrisa, Kelly, Martin and Larry.

Thank you to the JIT team for all the awesome feedback. A new series is always exciting and nerve-wracking.

Michael and I thought we had a great idea for a new world, but we don't really know until we get objective feedback. What would I do without all you awesome readers?

Thank you to my friends and family. Writing is a strange profession. I work weird hours, talk to myself, have a strange diet, get antsy about deadlines. But the wonderful people in my life continue to show their encouragement and thoughtfulness no matter what. It is never lost on me because I know that I wouldn't be doing what I love without all you amazing people, cheering me on.

And as with all my books, the final thank you goes to my muse, Lydia. I wrote my first book so that I could make my daughter proud, and it's never stopped. I write every book for you, my love.

Sarah Noffke writes YA and NA science fiction, fantasy, paranormal and urban fantasy. In addition to being an author, she is a mother, podcaster and professor. Noffke holds a Masters of Management and teaches college business/writing courses. Most of her students have no idea that she toils away her hours crafting fictional characters. www.sarahnoffke.com

Check out other work by Sarah author here.

Ghost Squadron:

Formation #1:
   Kill the bad guys. Save the Galaxy. All in a hard day's work.
   After ten years of wandering the outer rim of the galaxy, Eddie Teach is a man without a purpose. He was one of the toughest pilots in the Federation, but now he's

just a regular guy, getting into bar fights and making a difference wherever he can. It's not the same as flying a ship and saving colonies, but it'll have to do.

That is, until General Lance Reynolds tracks Eddie down and offers him a job. There are bad people out there, plotting terrible things, killing innocent people, and destroying entire colonies. **Someone has to stop them.**

Eddie, along with the genetically-enhanced combat pilot Julianna Fregin and her trusty E.I. named Pip, must recruit a diverse team of specialists, both human and alien. They'll need to master their new Q-Ship, one of the most powerful strike ships ever constructed. And finally, they'll have to stop a faceless enemy so powerful, it threatens to destroy the entire Federation.

All in a day's work, right?

Experience this exciting military sci-fi saga and the latest addition to the expanded Kurtherian Gambit Universe. If you're a fan of Mass Effect, Firefly, or Star Wars, you'll love this riveting new space opera.

NOTE: If cursing is a problem, then this might not be for you.

Check out the entire series here.

The Precious Galaxy Series:

Corruption #1

A new evil lurks in the darkness.

After an explosion, the crew of a battlecruiser mysteriously disappears.

Bailey and Lewis, complete strangers, find themselves

suddenly onboard the damaged ship. Lewis hasn't worked a case in years, not since the final one broke his spirit and his bank account. The last thing Bailey remembers is preparing to take down a fugitive on Onyx Station.

Mysteries are harder to solve when there's no evidence left behind.

Bailey and Lewis don't know how they got onboard *Ricky Bobby* or why. However, they quickly learn that whatever was responsible for the explosion and disappearance of the crew is still on the ship.

Monsters are real and what this one can do changes everything.

The new team bands together to discover what happened and how to fight the monster lurking in the bottom of the battlecruiser.

Will they find the missing crew? Or will the monster end them all?

The Soul Stone Mage Series:

House of Enchanted #1:

The Kingdom of Virgo has lived in peace for thousands of years...until now.

The humans from Terran have always been real assholes to the witches of Virgo. Now a silent war is brewing, and the timing couldn't be worse. Princess Azure will soon be crowned queen of the Kingdom of Virgo.

In the Dark Forest a powerful potion-maker has been murdered.

Charmsgood was the only wizard who could stop a

deadly virus plaguing Virgo. He also knew about the devastation the people from Terran had done to the forest.

Azure must protect her people. Mend the Dark Forest. Create alliances with savage beasts. No biggie, right?

But on coronation day everything changes. Princess Azure isn't who she thought she was and that's a big freaking problem.

Welcome to The Revelations of Oriceran. Check out the entire series here.

The Lucidites Series:

Awoken, #1:
Around the world humans are hallucinating after sleepless nights.

In a sterile, underground institute the forecasters keep reporting the same events.

And in the backwoods of Texas, a sixteen-year-old girl is about to be caught up in a fierce, ethereal battle.

Meet Roya Stark. She drowns every night in her dreams, spends her hours reading classic literature to avoid her family's ridicule, and is prone to premonitions— which are becoming more frequent. And now her dreams are filled with strangers offering to reveal what she has always wanted to know: Who is she? That's the question that haunts her, and she's about to find out. But will Roya live to regret learning the truth?

Stunned, #2
Revived, #3

The Reverians Series:

Defects, #1:

In the happy, clean community of Austin Valley, everything appears to be perfect. Seventeen-year-old Em Fuller, however, fears something is askew. Em is one of the new generation of Dream Travelers. For some reason, the gods have not seen fit to gift all of them with their expected special abilities. Em is a Defect—one of the unfortunate Dream Travelers not gifted with a psychic power. Desperate to do whatever it takes to earn her gift, she endures painful daily injections along with commands from her overbearing, loveless father. One of the few bright spots in her life is the return of a friend she had thought dead—but with his return comes the knowledge of a shocking, unforgivable truth. The society Em thought was protecting her has actually been betraying her, but she has no idea how to break away from its authority without hurting everyone she loves.

Rebels, #2

Warriors, #3

Vagabond Circus Series:

Suspended, #1:

When a stranger joins the cast of Vagabond Circus—a circus that is run by Dream Travelers and features real magic—mysterious events start happening. The once orderly grounds of the circus become riddled with hidden threats. And the ringmaster realizes not only are his circus and its magic at risk, but also his very life.

Vagabond Circus caters to the skeptics. Without skeptics, it would close its doors. This is because Vagabond

Circus runs for two reasons and only two reasons: first and foremost to provide the lost and lonely Dream Travelers a place to be illustrious. And secondly, to show the nonbelievers that there's still magic in the world. If they believe, then they care, and if they care, then they don't destroy. They stop the small abuse that day-by-day breaks down humanity's spirit. If Vagabond Circus makes one skeptic believe in magic, then they halt the cycle, just a little bit. They allow a little more love into this world. That's Dr. Dave Raydon's mission. And that's why this ringmaster recruits. That's why he directs. That's why he puts on a show that makes people question their beliefs. He wants the world to believe in magic once again.

Paralyzed, #2

Released, #3

Ren Series:

Ren: The Man Behind the Monster, #1:

Born with the power to control minds, hypnotize others, and read thoughts, Ren Lewis, is certain of one thing: God made a mistake. No one should be born with so much power. A monster awoke in him the same year he received his gifts. At ten years old. A prepubescent boy with the ability to control others might merely abuse his powers, but Ren allowed it to corrupt him. And since he can have and do anything he wants, Ren should be happy. However, his journey teaches him that harboring so much power doesn't bring happiness, it steals it. Once this realization sets in, Ren makes up his mind to do the one thing that can bring his tortured soul some peace. He must kill the monster.

Note This book is NA and has strong language, violence and sexual references.

Ren: God's Little Monster, #2
Ren: The Monster Inside the Monster, #3
Ren: The Monster's Adventure, #3.5
Ren: The Monster's Death

Olento Research Series:

Alpha Wolf, #1:
Twelve men went missing.

Six months later they awake from drug-induced stupors to find themselves locked in a lab.

And on the night of a new moon, eleven of those men, possessed by new—and inhuman—powers, break out of their prison and race through the streets of Los Angeles until they disappear one by one into the night.

Olento Research wants its experiments back. Its CEO, Mika Lenna, will tear every city apart until he has his werewolves imprisoned once again. He didn't undertake a huge risk just to lose his would-be assassins.

However, the Lucidite Institute's main mission is to save the world from injustices. Now, it's Adelaide's job to find these mutated men and protect them and society, and fast. Already around the nation, wolflike men are being spotted. Attacks on innocent women are happening. And then, Adelaide realizes what her next step must be: She has to find the alpha wolf first. Only once she's located him can she stop whoever is behind this experiment to create wild beasts out of human beings.

Lone Wolf, #2

Rabid Wolf, #3

Bad Wolf, #4

BOOKS BY MICHAEL ANDERLE

For a complete list of books by Michael Anderle, please visit:

www.lmbpn.com/ma-books/

All LMBPN Audiobooks are Available at Audible.com and iTunes

To see all LMBPN audiobooks, including those written by
Michael Anderle please visit:

www.lmbpn.com/audible

CONNECT WITH THE AUTHORS

Connect with Sarah and sign up for her email list here:

http://www.sarahnoffke.com/connect/

You can catch her podcast, LA Chicks, here:

http://lachicks.libsyn.com/

Connect with Michael Anderle and sign up for his email list here:

Website: http://lmbpn.com

Email List: http://lmbpn.com/email/

Facebook:
www.facebook.com/TheKurtherianGambitBooks

www.ingramcontent.com/pod-product-compliance
Lightning Source LLC
Chambersburg PA
CBHW022024120726
47898CB00007BA/2115